OPERATOR 5:
BLOOD REIGN OF THE DICTATOR

BLOOD REIGN
OF THE DICTATOR

By Curtis Steele

STEEGER BOOKS • 2020

PUBLISHING HISTORY

"Blood Reign of the Dictator" originally appeared in the May, 1935 (Vol. 4, No. 2) issue of *Operator #5* magazine. Copyright © 2020 by Argosy Communications, Inc. All rights reserved.

CHAPTER 1
EXECUTIONS IN SECRET

C OUPLINGS CLASHED along the length of the freight train as it jarred to a stop outside the great city of Hartland. Its trucks screeched under hard clamped brake shoes; the locomotive sneezed out steam, and like a tired, almost human monster stood snorting and panting.

It was an unusual stop: the country hereabouts was wooded, lonely, and filled with the blackness of midnight. The lights of the metropolis still lay far ahead.

But this train, though a string of empties, was freighted with the destiny of a great nation.

Two grimy figures huddled in the darkness beneath one of the boxcars—two secret passengers who clung precariously to the sooty rods. Throughout the long night they had crouched in their dangerous position, while ties streamed beneath them, while ponderous iron trucks clicked over fishplates, and rails shrieked a song, two feet below them, of endlessly impending peril. Their faces were caked with grime; their eyes stung with the bite of the wind. Their clothing was ragged, patched, filthy.... Yet they were destined to remake the fate of the United States of America!

With the halt, their nerves tightened warily. A gleam of light startled them. Still clinging to the greasy rods, they peered across the embankment, into the black wood that spread beyond.

Through the trees two spots of light moved like the flaming eyes of a giant dragon on the prowl. There was a clanking and snorting, the sound of a heavy truck crawling over a rough road. As it snarled around a bend and into clearer view, they saw that armed men were aboard it.

Two uniformed guards rode the roof of the truck, gripping rifles in their hands. Two others, similarly armed, clung with

their free hands to the running boards. The garb of all four was as black as the night itself; they wore visored helmets which left even their faces masked in shadow.

A heavy sedan followed the truck around the bend. In it sat five uniformed men—one of whom wore the silver shoulder decorations of a United States Army officer.

And in all the world, no eyes save those of the two disreputable, secret freight passengers saw that strange military detachment probing its way deep into the woods on its mission of mystery.

They continued to watch, as both cars stopped in a clearing. The soldiers hastened from the sedan and, at the ringing command of their officer, held their rifles ready for quick action. The others, who had ridden in the truck, leaped down, unlocked its heavy rear doors and swung them open. From the officer came a snappy order:

"Prisoners, descend!"

OUT OF the utter blackness of the truck interior stepped a mild-seeming man with snow-white hair, garbed in a costly business suit. An elderly woman came next, her manner dignified and bewildered. Third to appear was a young man, whose face showed chalk-white in the reflected shine of the truck's headlamps. Fourth came a portly man with a florid, honest-looking face, dressed in the blue uniform of a municipal policeman. Lastly appeared a girl—a girl in her twenties, unusually pretty, who hurried to the side of the young man, her eyes sparkling, her chin raised defiantly. In the dim shine of the clearing they stood in a silent group, ringed by the soldiers in black uniform, facing the glittering rifles.

"Fall in!"

The black squad immediately formed around the prisoners. A second command sent them marching past the truck—the uniformed men smartly, the prisoners out of step and confused. All moved into the glare of the headlights, and at another order stopped, about-faced, and blinked in the blinding beams. The officer, who had followed, sent the black squad marching back then, and once more about-faced them, so that the uniformed men and the white-faced captives confronted each other across the lonesome clearing.

The officer drew a document from his pocket and in low, stern tones read from it.

"By virtue of the power vested in him by the will of the people, by executive order of the Commander-in-Chief, and under Article One Hundred of the Code of Protection of the sovereign State of New Cornwall, the following prisoners of the State are commanded to suffer the penalty of death, to be executed upon them as punishment for the high crime of Treason committed against the State."

Then, so swiftly that no syllable was intelligible, the squad-officer read a list of names, finishing with that affixed to the warrant of death.

The pale prisoners spoke no word. The officer carefully folded a spotless white handkerchief, stepped toward the elderly woman, gestured as though to tie it about her eyes.

With cold pride, she pushed it away. The officer stepped next toward the girl; she too refused the bandage. One after another, the condemned declined to blanket their eyes from the rifle squad which faced them. The officer stepped back grimly.

And still, from the shadows beneath the boxcar, the two startled tramps watched in stunned and chilled amazement.

"Ready!"

The black squad stood stiff, erect, shadowed against the glare of light which spotted the condemned five.

"Aim!"

Rifles snapped to black-clothed shoulders, leveling with ominous precision at the group before them.

"Fire!"

A spiteful, clattering burst rocked across the clearing. Flame blazed from the rifles. Bullets thudded into the bodies of the five huddled, waiting figures. And as powder smoke wafted above the lighted clearing—the five fell, a crumpled heap of dead.

IN GRIM unbelief the two hoboes peered from under the boxcar at the five who had died. The scene before their eyes was an incredible distortion of reality—and yet vividly, appallingly real. It was as though, for the moment, they had been transported to a European nation terrorized by the despotic power, the bloody "purges" of a militaristic dictator. Yet this spot was located just outside the capital of one of the forty-eight United States! Before their eyes, in "the land of the free," an execution had taken place—in secret!

"Bury them!"

The command rang from the grim-voiced officer. The black squad broke ranks, hurried to the truck, and with shovels and picks hastened back to the spot where bullets had torn away five lives.

The swinging blades of the black squad deepened a cavity in the earth. Heartlessly, they dragged the bodies of the dead toward it. As though at a common, obscene signal, they dropped their tools and fell upon the bodies like vultures. Their dirt-caked

fingers tore a necklace from the
dead throat of the elderly woman,
rings from the hand of the girl,
wallets from the pockets of the
men. They stuffed their loot into
their tunics. Then, their vandalism
finished, they pulled the dead into the common grave, covered it.

At the officer's command, the black-uniformed men sprang
into the truck. The doors closed. The powerful motor snorted.
As the truck backed, the sedan spurted away, carrying the officer from the scene. The truck went crawling laboriously over the
road. The gleam of its headlights glimmered away among the
trees. The last shine vanished; the last sound blended away into
the quieted breathing of the locomotive.

And in unmarked earth, shrouded by the blackness of
midnight, lay the five who had died.

On the rods of the boxcar, one of the two huddled figures
moved. He whispered, "Stay here!" and dropped to the ground.
Ducking into the open, he heeled down the embankment,
groped his way into the clearing. At the spot of raw earth where
the dead now lay buried, he paused. His one filthy hand tore the
greasy, misshapen hat from his head. His lips pressed hard and
grim upon words which were scarcely a breath.

"You will not be forgotten!"

From the locomotive, far up the tracks, steam burst again.
Hurriedly the unkempt figure pulled a small electric torch from
his pocket, swung its circle around the earth-sprinkled grass. He
steadied it; then, stooping, picked up an object which the bright

spot had disclosed. It was a wallet, emptied of money by the predatory fingers of one of the black squad—but still containing, as he discovered the next instant, an identification card.

Upon it the hobo read the name of one of the five who had died.

A series of metallic crashes jarred along the string of empty boxcars, and the locomotive began to move. The tramp stuffed the abandoned wallet into his pocket, sprinted across the clearing. Springing up the embankment he pulled himself upon the rods, beside his companion, just as the advance of the engine was transmitted to the car. Again the rails began to stream along underneath as the freight resumed its journey to the great city of Hartland, New Cornwall.

Hands gripping the rods, he peered back at the clearing—at the unmarked grave where lay five who had suffered a secret execution—until the shifting screen of woods blocked it from view.

THE FREIGHT crawled into a spider web of tracks in the vast railroad yards of the Hartland Grand Terminal Station, and again stopped. Quickly its two secret passengers crawled off the rods, one carrying a battered, peeling suitcase. They hurried through the darkness, alert to avoid the yard detectives, keeping to the deepest shadows.

The tramp who had found the wallet led the way toward a string of Pullman cars which stood idle, awaiting the dispatcher's orders. He was in his middle twenties. His companion was a boy of about fourteen. Grime masked the characteristics of both faces, but the soot-rimmed eyes of each were alert and sharp.

At the steps of a Pullman they paused, glanced around warily, then darted up the steps. Making sure the car was empty, they stepped, together into the men's washroom. The elder of the two pulled the window shades, lighted his torch, placed it on a towel shelf. By its light he unclasped the lid of his worn suitcase. Quickly he made the first moves of a procedure that was to effect an amazing transformation.

With a special soap, brought from the case, he scrubbed his hands and face clean of the greasy road grime. In the light his face was revealed as finely chiseled, strong, purely American in cast.

As he rinsed his hands, a peculiar scar was uncovered on the back of his right hand—a marking of black and white and gray shaped uncannily like a spread-winged American eagle.

At a second wash bowl his companion, the boy of fourteen, was doing likewise. The boy's face shone in the gleam, his cheeks freckled, his nose pugnacious.

They stripped off their filthy clothing, took suits from the case. A few moments transformed the young man from a disreputable tramp into an impeccably dressed figure. He tugged a soft felt on his head at a jaunty angle; flicked specks of dust from his mirror-bright shoes; adjusted the spotless, starched cuffs of his shirt; tucked a colorful handkerchief into his breast pocket. Lastly, he hung across his vest a chain to which a strange ornament was affixed.

It was a death's-head cunningly fashioned of gold, and its eyes glittered ruby fire.

Meanwhile the boy placed on his left hand a ring of white

9

metal, on which a white skull was emblazoned against a black background. It pictured the young man's watch-charm; and on the forehead of the skull the mystic numeral 5 was engraved.

Working swiftly, they stored their filthy clothing in the old suitcase, then ventured out to the steps of the Pullman. Tossing the grip away, they hurried across a maze of tracks to a landing platform, strode briskly through a gate. In the center of the great terminal, above the swarm of people, great red-painted signs rose.

YOUNG FOR PRESIDENT!

VOTE AGAINST POVERTY BY VOTING FOR YOUNG!

REBEL AGAINST HIGH TAXES—VOTE FOR YOUNG!

YOUNG AND PROSPERITY—GIVE THEM YOUR VOTE!

AT THE far side of the vast room a platform had been erected, and around it the thickest crowd had gathered. Through a public-address system a thick-necked man was roaring the eloquent exhortations of a campaign speech. His words thundered under the vaulted rotunda.

"Citizens! The day after tomorrow your votes will transform Governor Young of New Cornwall into President Young of the United States! The voice of a hundred-million inspired people will rise to proclaim to the world that Ursus Young, and Ursus Young alone, can direct our nation back to prosperity. The United States can save itself from complete economic destruction only when President Young takes supreme command!"

The young man and the boy strode across the marble floor toward the exit marked, in shining letters, *Young Hotel.*

"Young's record as Governor of New Cornwall proves his unequaled ability to save the United States from chaos, from the blunderings of short-sighted bureaucrats!" The raucous voice went on. "He has abolished poverty in this great state! He has shifted the burden of taxation from the shoulders of the poor to the shoulders of the rich. He has regimented our industry so that now New Cornwall enjoys higher prosperity than any other state of the union! He has eliminated unemployment, and established old-age pensions. One man alone can strike away the cancers eating at the heart of America—and that man is Ursus Young!"

As the speaker paused, the young man, his eyes shining darkly, said in a quiet, yet bitter tone to the boy:

"One man alone, in the United States, would dare to order a merciless execution of those who have actively combated his regime of terroristic despotism."

He strode briskly through the lobby, his companion still alongside, and stopped by the desk. On every wall hung great banners, flaunting the name of Young for the Presidency. The voice of the speaker in the terminal was being reproduced from

11

a huge radio in the center of the foyer. Around it a crowd of men was listening:

"Governor Young has displayed his high courage, his rare leadership, in the admirable way in which he has marshaled his forces to battle the plague which has fallen upon this state. Keeping always in mind the common good, he has stopped at nothing to stamp out the death-dealing epidemic."

The young man and the boy had paused, and were eyeing a sign which rested on an easel in front of the desk. The sign read:

WARNING! Through Governor Young's Health Control Regulations, it is required that newcomers to all cities in the state must undergo a medical examination and carry a Certificate of Health. We can rent rooms only to persons so equipped. Anyone not possessing a Certificate is subject to instant arrest, deportation from the State, or imprisonment in a State Institution.

Beneath this startling notice a second had been tacked:

Residents of New Cornwall will not be permitted to enter any polling place and vote in the national Presidential election without their Certificates of Health.

At the desk the young man spoke to the clerk. "Is there any mail for Huntley Walsh?"

Taking the one letter the clerk handed him, he stepped aside, quickly ripped it open, removed a brief note and a newspaper clipping. The note read:

No word has yet been received from Diane Elliot. She was last seen leaving the Amalgamated Press Bureau in Hartland, N.C., two days ago. Her first dispatch, after her trip to Hartland from New York to write a series of expose articles on Governor Young's terrorism for the Amalgamated, is enclosed. She has simply vanished off the face of the earth.

That there is a connection between her disappearance and the lead article she wrote is a certainty.

Use utmost caution while in Hartland and avoid all possible danger.

Z-7.

THE YOUNG man, who had identified himself as Huntley Walsh, glanced quickly at the newspaper clipping. Its startling black headline declared:

SOVIET TERROR IN U.S. IS YOUNG'S WEAPON!
CRUSHES OPPONENTS, CONTROLS ALL STATE AGENCIES,
STAMPS OUT ALL FREEDOM!

Beneath was the line: *By Diane Elliot, Special Reporter for the Amalgamated Press.*

"Surrounding himself with gorilla bodyguards," the article began, "striking at his opponents through a terrifying system of secret police; dominating the courts, the police system, the lawmaking bodies; brushing aside all principles of American liberty, Governor Ursus Young of New Cornwall declares:

"I am the State!"

"This man, who has proclaimed, 'My word is the law'—this

man who has made himself virtual king of a commonwealth by bribery, coercion, and terror—this man who is looting his own state treasury—this man who has made a mockery of the words justice and right and democracy—this is the man who has bludgeoned his way into being made a candidate for the Presidency of the United States.

"Will he say, if the voters of the United States elect him to that office, 'I am the Nation!'?

"If Ursus Young is elected President of the United States, its people will find themselves ruled by a dictatorship more inhuman than that of Soviet Russia; they will see a reign of terror such as we have never yet known; they will become the prey of a mercilessly selfish demagogue; they will witness all the fine traditions of our country scrapped by his political chicanery.

"The dread Article of Emergency 100—a law railroaded through the State Senate by Governor Young—which puts into his hands a weapon by which he can exile or even condemn to death all who fight his political despotism—may be followed by a new Federal Article of Emergency which will give him absolute power of life or death over any person in the United States—a power to be executed at his merest whim!

"The Amalgamated Press today begins this series of amazing articles, presenting proof that the election of Ursus Young to the Presidency would mean the greatest disaster that ever befell the United States."

The eyes of the young man, who had identified himself as Huntley Walsh, lifted swiftly as he heard steps near him. Across the lobby two uniformed men were striding—men wearing black uniforms like those of the execution squad! On their arms were bands labeled *Health Corps.* They were armed, and their faces were hard, brutally ugly.

They grasped the arms of a man who had just bought a newspaper at the lobby counter. First his kindly eyes lighted in surprise; then his face went pale with dread.

"Your Health Certificate?" one of the uniformed men demanded gruffly.

"I have my certificate—but I am a physician. I have offered my services to Governor Young. I do not follow him politically, but I am doing everything possible to cooperate with the quarantine." The doctor removed a red card from his wallet, proffered it.

The Health Corpsman who had spoken scarcely glanced at it. "Forged!" he declared. Swiftly he tore the card to bits. "You're under arrest!"

THE PHYSICIAN swayed as if he had been struck bodily. "There's some mistake!" he protested. "I obtained my card from the Chief of Public Health at the State House. I watched him sign it!"

The two uniformed men gripped his arms tightly. "You're under arrest—don't argue! Come with us!"

The doctor's face grew even whiter. "This is a trumped-up charge!" he cried. "You're arresting me because I refused to vote for such a scoundrel as Young. His damned Cheka reported me because I'm working to prevent his election. You can't—"

"You're resisting arrest!"

The bigger of the two armed men pulled a blackjack from

15

his hip pocket. Glimpsing it, the doctor drew back in terror, wrenched free of the hands gripping him.

"I'm damned if I'll go with you! I'm on my way to see a patient who is dangerously ill. You'll place his life in danger if you—"

The two men snatched at him again. The physician whirled away. Fear shining in his eyes, he ran stumblingly toward the main exit.

Instantly, both Health Corpsmen drew revolvers. They sprang after the fleeing man, jerked up their weapons, aimed point-blank at his back.

The young man known as Huntley Walsh started forward abruptly—but as abruptly, checked by an inner warning, he halted.

Blasting shots rocked the lobby as the guns in the hands of both black-uniformed men blazed fire. The glass of the main entrance spattered, the physician whirled half around, and an expression of abject disbelief came in his eyes. Tottering against the broken pane, he clawed at his chest, dropped to his knees, then spilled to the floor. His hat fell off, disclosing two wounds at the back of his head which glistened in the light—glistened red.

His newspaper, too, had fallen. And as he lay there in a crumpled heap, the paper's black headlines proclaimed mockingly:

YOUNG'S ELECTION CERTAIN. MARTIAL LAW FIGHTS
PLAGUE UNDER GOVERNOR'S COMMAND.

The two armed men whipped around, their guns leveled. The explosions had shocked the very air. Civilians stood motionless,

16

silent and pale. There was no sound save the voice issuing from the radio, a voice which boomed with bombastic, florid phrases:

"President Young… the savior of the people… the leader of millions… the friend of all!"

And in the lobby of Young's hotel a medical soldier of mercy lay dead—killed by the bullets of Young's Corpsmen.

Even now one of the killers cried: "He resisted arrest—you all saw it! He had the first stages of the plague. Lucky for all of you we got him, or you and your families would catch it from him. The welfare of the State is at stake!"

Out of the radio roared a burst of cheering and applause. The crowd near the distant microphone was hailing the leadership of Governor Young. But those in the lobby winced before the menace of the guns in the hands of the Corpsmen. Tearing their eyes from the still form on the floor, they began to hasten out the exits.

From the desk, two employees of the hotel hurried over to the dead man. They lifted the body, carried it away through a door—and a crimson blot remained on the floor. While the lobby emptied, while the raucous cheering thundered from the radio, the young man known as Huntley Walsh watched with darkened eyes.

"Careful, Tim!" he warned his companion in a cautious whisper. "This state is like a foreign nation within the borders of the United States. It's as dangerous for us here as though we were spies in enemy country in time of war. Take absolutely no chances!"

CHAPTER 2
PLAGUE OF THE KING

THE YOUNG man known as Huntley Walsh strode across the lobby to a telephone booth. The boy he had called Tim stood outside the door, alertly watching, while he put through a long-distance call. The number he gave the operator was known only to a few men in the United States; the connections went through quickly. The answer came from Washington, D.C., hundreds of miles away.

"Mr. Quintus calling Mr. Sept."

"One moment." A throaty, quick voice followed the first. "Mr. Sept on the wire, Mr. Quintus."

"I have reached my destination."

"You are safe?"

"Yes, but—" Walsh hesitated, his eyes narrowing. "Quite safe, so far. I am about to execute my orders. Have you heard nothing else from—the girl?"

"No word whatever. I realize you are greatly concerned about her, but I must remind you that your orders are of first importance."

"Yes." The young man's lips tightened. His voice dropped. "Chief, I have a report of the utmost importance. Tonight I saw an example of the terrorism that will run rife over the country if—" Again he broke off.

"Yes?" the voice in Washington urged.

Huntley Walsh had heard a slight click on the wire. He had heard the one word "Yes?" more weakly than those previously

spoken to him over the line. His nerves
went hot when he said, cryptically:

"Thirteen."

It was a prearranged signal. It meant:
*Take warning! Someone has cut into the
line! Our conversation is being overheard.
We dare not continue!*

URSUS YOUNG

The voice from Washington said
blandly: "Thirteen is a satisfactory price.
I'll wait for further word from you."

"That's fine. Goodnight."

Walsh's face was a picture of anxiety as he stepped from the
booth. He noted men and women drifting into the lobby. Bell-
boys were hurrying away from the entrance; only a wet area
shone on the floor where the red of blood had blotted it. There,
on that spot, a man had died before a despot's guns, and now all
traces of his death had been wiped away.

At the curb in front of the hotel, Huntley Walsh stepped
into a taxi.

"The home of William Stockard," he directed the driver.

The man at the wheel jerked terrified eyes backward. "Nothin'
doin', buddy!" he blurted. "I won't take you to that place!"

Walsh removed his wallet from his pocket and a ten-dollar
bill from the wallet. "The home of William Stockard—quickly,"
he insisted.

The driver's head wagged. "I ain't goin' to run the chance of
takin' you there! I'm warnin' you to stay away from that place. I
wouldn't go."

Walsh added two more bills to the first, and an ominous ring edged his voice. "To the home of William Stockard, as fast as you can make it."

The driver blinked. Unwillingly, he took the money. "I'll take you to the nearest corner, but that's all. If the Blacks see me, I'll just turn up missin', that's all. You better not go there. You can't get in anyway, and if—"

"Start! Now!"

THE SHARP command sent the taxi swinging into the street. The driver wagged his head as though humoring a madman.

As the cab spurted into traffic, Walsh and the boy gazed curiously out the windows. Everywhere placards, banners, and streamers, carrying the name of Young as Candidate for the Presidency, were in evidence. On street corners, speakers were haranguing the crowds. Patrolling the streets were scores and hundreds of the black-uniformed men wearing armbands identifying them as members of various state agencies. Hysterical cries of approval rang from the mobs on the corners in response to flowery phrases of the speakers. And yet there was a tension in the air—the tension induced by terror.

Speeding through a residential section, Huntley Walsh noted that even here, where there were no crowds, the Black Troopers were patrolling. Others, leaning on rifles, were stationed in front of numerous houses—on the doors of which were tacked red placards reading QUARANTINED.

When the cab paused at a red light, Walsh saw the door of a house burst open and light stream out. Three black-uniformed men appeared, dragging a civilian across the sill. After the prisoner hurried a woman who strove frantically to tear him free, and from within the house a small girl watched in white-faced fear.

Ruthlessly the Black Troopers wrestled their captive off the porch, into a waiting car. Immediately it spurted away, directly past the red light, whereupon the woman collapsed on the curb, sobbing.

Quietly Walsh asked his driver: "What has happened there?"

"Don't ask questions! Nobody asks questions about what happens. If you do—"

Into the fearful silence that completed the sentence Walsh said: "I have heard it remarked that the plague—the peculiar plague which has struck chiefly in the state of New Cornwall—attacks only those who are not friendly to Governor Young. Those who pander to him are, somehow, immune."

"God—don't say that!" The driver peered around in terror. "There're secret police everywhere! If one of 'em heard you say that—God!"

"Would I—disappear?"

The frantic eyes of the man at the wheel implored silence. The cab started up again, sped along. It swung around corners dizzily, as though the driver were hotly anxious to rid himself of his dangerous fares. When, at last, it swerved to the curb at a corner, the driver blurted: "There it is—the big house. I can't take you any closer! Better stay away from it!"

The taxi whirled from sight at the next corner, the fading glare of its lights leaving Walsh and the boy standing in deep shadow. They gazed across the street, at a massive house surrounded by

21

gardens and enclosed by an ivy-covered stone wall. Only a few of its windows showed light. At its front entrance two black-uniformed men stood on guard. Upon the wall a glaring red placard announced that the residence was quarantined.

The boy was peering into his companion's face anxiously. "Gee, Jimmy—did you mean it?" he asked. "That if we're caught, we'll be treated like spies in a foreign country?"

"We have no identity cards. We smuggled ourselves into this state because we could not pass the frontier guards in any other way. We will be dealt with summarily if we're caught— sentenced without a trial, by the secret police. I told you, Tim, when we started, that it was dangerous."

"I know, Jimmy! I'm not afraid—except for you. You're taking a terrible chance!"

"No more than you, Tim." Huntley Walsh's lips tightened. "We saw five persons executed tonight, exactly as though at the command of a bloody European dictator. We saw another man shot down in cold blood. I called the Chief, and immediately the telephone line was tapped. No telegrams can be sent without the approval of the so-called Communications Commis-

JIMMY CHRISTOPHER

sion. No one can enter the state by train, plane, or automobile without being thoroughly scrutinized and having his destination recorded. Yet this is not Russia or Germany—this is one of the United States of America!"

"Jimmy—what're you going to do here?"

"Try to find Diane—but first of all I must follow orders. Inside that house is a man whom the Chief ordered me to see. I am going to see him—now."

23

HUNTLEY WALSH crossed the street briskly, following the stone wall with the alert boy at his side, until he drifted into a mass of deep shadows. He paused, glanced around warily. From a point beyond the corner came the sound of gritting heels—a black-uniformed sentry on patrol. Walsh whispered quickly:

"Across the street, Tim—and watch sharp! If I don't come back within an hour, you slip away. Try to get out of the state without being seen and communicate as quickly as possible with Z-7. Tell him, exactly, everything that has happened. Hurry, Tim!"

"Gee, Jimmy!" The boy blurted in his anxiety, but whirled and sped across the street as his companion sidled to the wall.

Quickly Huntley Walsh lifted himself to the top of the barrier. He glanced back, to make sure the boy was out of sight, then dropped down. At the edge of a garden, in deep shadow, he paused, peering across the dark grounds. The place was silent… the grass had grown rank; the flowering bushes were untended; an air of desolation hung about the huge residence. And at the gate, ominous shadows, the armed guards stood their posts.

Walsh darted across the grounds, to the rear of the house. He paused at a door lighted dimly by a glow shining through a kitchen window. On the panels a red card was tacked, and beneath the warning word QUARANTINE was a block of smaller type.

> All persons are warned that violation of this quarantine will be punished by summary arrest and imprisonment. No one may legally enter this domicile except properly accredited State Physicians.

The name appended was that of Ursus Young, Governor of the State of New Cornwall.

Huntley Walsh knocked.

Quick footfalls responded, came to the door and stopped. A quavering voice asked through the panels: "Who is it?"

"A friend."

"But—no one can come in here! Go away!"

"Unless you admit me," Huntley Walsh answered firmly, "I will force my way in."

From inside came a startled exclamation. Then a chain rattled; a crack opened; the eye of an old man looked out.

Walsh unceremoniously pushed the door open and stepped in. The old manservant recoiled in fright.

"Do not be afraid," Walsh urged briskly. "I am acting in Mr. Stockard's best interests. I am aware of the chances I'm taking by entering this house, but I'm quite determined to take them. I wish to see Mr. Stockard at once."

"It's impossible! Mr. Stockard is seriously ill with the plague. I have been his servant for fifty years, sir, but I have never seen anything as frightful as his affliction. The doctors can do nothing. If you come near him, you may contract it and—"

"Haven't you thought it strange," Walsh asked quietly, "that you, who are near Mr. Stockard continually, have not contracted it?"

"I only know—"

"Take me to Mr. Stockard at once!" Into Huntley Walsh's voice came the imperative ring which brooked no argument, no delay.

The old manservant turned with a wag of his head and shambled to a door at the end of a long hallway. Hand on the knob, the old servant peered at Walsh a moment—a moment of silence which permeated the dwelling with an evil spell.

"Who shall I say, sir?"

"Say a young man who knows of and sympathizes completely with Mr. Stockard's past attacks upon Governor Young."

The door opened upon a dim light and closed. Huntley Walsh waited, while voices rumbled inside the room. Again the door opened. He strode in and, stopping short just over the sill, stared, appalled.

Slumped in a deep-cushioned chair at the other end of the room, was a man. Blankets were wrapped around him, so that only his face lay exposed to the shaded light—and it was a face parched by a devastating fever. The cheeks were sunken; the skin was horribly blotched; the eyes glittered with an unnatural brightness in their withered sockets. In that chair sat a shrunken mummy of a man tortured by a frightful sickness.

HUNTLEY WALSH had, in the past, seen William Stockard several times. Stockard had been a great newspaper publisher then, his dynamic energy and unflagging mind controlling the destiny of a string of the most powerful dailies in the state of New Cornwall. Walsh remembered a man of powerful frame, of strapping strength, of admirable personal presence and great charm. Yet the William Stockard he faced now was a ghastly shadow of that other man.

Walsh's eyes glowed darkly as he approached the big chair. Stockard's too bright eyes studied him fearfully. Walsh extended his firm hand, and Stockard's skeleton one trembled into it—a hand burning hot, horribly mottled, so weak that, once released, it dropped back immediately within the blankets. The man spoke in a voice—not resonant and commanding, as Walsh had once heard it—but with the quavering whisper of a terrified mind.

"What do—you want?"

The young man's answer was to remove a flat silver case from his inner pocket. He pressed upon a concealed spring in the corner, and a paper-thin leaf sprang up. Inside the case a letter was framed. The eyes of William Stockard widened upon it as he read:

THE WHITE HOUSE

Washington

To Whom It May Concern:

The identity of the bearer of this letter must be kept strictly confidential.

He is Operator 5 of the United States Intelligence Service.

The signature affixed to the document was that of the President of the United States.

Stockard's voice rose in a terrified cackle. "For God's sake, go away! Leave this house! Leave this city—this state! Go away now—now!—or you'll die as horribly as I am dying!"

Operator 5—whose unparalleled achievements in the Intelligence Service were recorded in its archives under the name of James Christopher—drew a chair close to the emaciated man.

"I have no intention of leaving," he said firmly. "I am here upon orders of my Chief. I am detailed to investigate this strange plague which strikes down the enemies of Governor Young but not his friends. I want to learn from you, sir—because I know you to be a thoroughly honest and fearless man—the true condition of this state."

Stockard was trembling within the enwrapping blankets; his gaunt eyes were shining with fevered brilliance. "Fearless—! Once, perhaps—once, when I was a man! But not now. God, you don't realize what a chance you are taking! The secret police are everywhere—spying on everyone—Governor Young's Cheka! My own servant may be one of them. The doctor who is upstairs now may be one of them. I am afraid of them all—and you call me fearless!"

Jimmy Christopher's eyes narrowed. "The plague has done this to you?"

"Yes—this horrible disease! It has wasted me away—this fever. It's a terrible fever. I've had it night and day for weeks, a fever that's burning me up. My doctor has established a laboratory upstairs to help me. I'm taking the medicines prescribed by him and the Chief of Public Health—the only medicine that can stop it—and yet it doesn't stop! It's consuming me alive!"

OPERATOR 5 reached to a taboret beside the chair, lifted a bottle containing a yellow fluid. The bottle bore no label, and the liquid was odorless, shining like yellow amber in the light.

"That's the medicine—the only one that can help me—yet which doesn't help. The Chief of Public Health has made exhaustive researches; he's found that this alone helps sufferers of the plague. No one knows what the disease is, but this medicine has helped others. And every day I hope for improvement—yet every day my condition becomes worse!"

Operator 5 said briskly: "With your permission, Mr. Stockard…."

Stockard gazed in fascination as Operator 5 placed a few drops of the solution on his tongue. It had a bitter taste.

From his pocket he removed a small leather case containing long, thin vials, half of them empty, the others filled with labeled chemical reagents. He poured some of the medicine into one of the

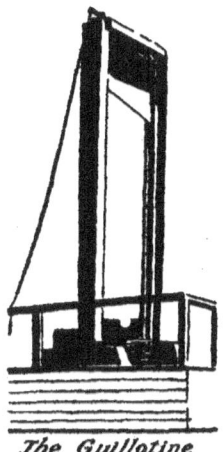

The Guillotine

tubes, quickly added a few drops of several of the chemicals.

At the addition of the first, the yellow turned to a blood red. The second faded all color from it. The third turned the colorless liquid black as ink. Briskly, then, Operator 5 corked the specimen, and closed his case.

"Mr. Stockard, I have reason to believe—"

A step at the door interrupted. The man who strode into the room was exceedingly tall; his lean arms were grotesquely long. He brought up short upon seeing Operator 5, and his big-jointed hand rose to stroke his Vandyke beard. He frowned ominously as Stockard said quaveringly:

"Dr. Hurwit, a friend of mine, Mr.—Mr. Carter."

Dr. Hurwit strode forward suddenly. "Mr. Carter, you have violated quarantine. That, sir, is a serious offense. As a Special Health Officer of Governor Young's Plague Control Board, I must place you under arrest. Furthermore, I will require you to remain in this house until I am satisfied that you have not contracted the disease."

Quietly Jimmy Christopher answered: "I am quite positive, Dr. Hurwit, that I have not contracted the plague."

"I will examine you in a moment," the physician declared flatly. "Mr. Stockard, I have determined to double the dose of your medicine. It's time to take it now. I think I can promise you that you will be well soon if—here you are."

Dr. Hurwit, while speaking, had uncorked the bottle of yellow liquid and poured a tablespoonful. He extended it toward his patient; Stockard made ready to take it eagerly.

Operator 5, his lips tightening grimly, stepped forward. His hand struck the spoon, sent the golden stuff spattering across the room.

While Stockard gasped, Dr. Hurwit straightened in cold fury. "Sir! How dare you—!"

"Your medicine will never cure this case of so-called plague, Doctor," Operator 5 declared coldly. "Quite the contrary. Your prescription is *causing* your patient's extremely high fever."

"What! You know nothing about it!" The doctor's eyes blazed; his face crimsoned with fury. "If you interfere again, I'll order you sent to a State institution—and see that you're kept there!"

"You *may* not know that your medicine is actually the cause of Mr. Stockard's sickness. But I think you do, Doctor," Operator 5 insisted levelly. "You decided to double his dose… why? To hasten his death?"

"I am trying to save this man's life! You're talking like a madman—"

OPERATOR 5'S sibilant command broke into the physician's words: "Listen! If you attempt to give Mr. Stockard another dose of that stuff, I'll keep you from doing it—forcibly—and you can make all the threats you please. The fact is, your medicine is a solution of alpha-dinitrophenol."

Dr. Hurwit sputtered: "Impossible!"

"Not impossible, Doctor. True." Jimmy Christopher took the bottle into his hand. "If you will allow me to come into your laboratory I'll repeat my analysis on a larger scale and prove it beyond all doubt. You know, do you not, Doctor, that alpha-dinitrophenol is a coal-tar product akin to picric acid, that a dose of it seven one-millionths the weight of the patient steps up the rate of metabolism as high as fifty percent? The result is a devastating fever because the body is running at too high a speed—really burning itself up. Repeated doses of the stuff have literally aged Mr. Stockard before his time, exhausted him with fever—and further doses will kill him!"

Hurwit thundered an exclamation of rage. "Young man, you have made a serious charge against me! I intend to see the proof you offer. I know the tests for dinitrophenol—I have campaigned against fat-reducing mixtures which contain it. Come to my laboratory at once, sir, with that medicine, and I'll prove to you that you lie!"

The physician spun on his heel, swung his grotesquely long legs from the room. The door slapped shut with a resounding jar. Operator 5 felt the faltering, hot hand of William Stockard grasp his.

"Is it true? Have you told the truth? This stuff has caused this damnable fever?"

"There's not the slightest doubt in the world about it," Jimmy Christopher declared. "I'm amazed that it hasn't already burned the life out of you."

The flaring eyes of Stockard widened; his withered hand gripped Operator 5's more tightly. "I—I see it now! That's why Watkins hasn't caught the plague! That's why the fever doesn't abate! That's why Dr. Hurwit is here—not to help me, but to kill me—by order of Governor Young!"

"The one specific remedy offered by the Governor's Chief of Public Health," Jimmy Christopher declared with certainty, "is the one cause of the so-called plague!"

Stockard peered fearfully at the door. "Look out for that man!" he quavered. "He will not permit the truth to be known. Already he must be informing the secret police—perhaps Governor Young himself. Good God—you're in danger, my boy—in danger of your life! Leave while—"

"I want to know," Operator 5 insisted, "exactly what they have done to you, Mr. Stockard."

Stockard's parched lips drew tight. "This fever began soon after I had directed all my papers to oppose Young's nomination for the candidacy for President. While the national party convention was meeting here, in Hartland, I fought Young's machine. My voice was the only one raised against him. I was the only one who dared oppose him. I wrote the editorials myself—until I became so ill—"

STOCKARD'S HUSKY words quickened. "Young has jockeyed all my trusted men off my papers and put his hirelings in their places. I've been powerless to prevent his turning my papers into tub-thumping sheets for his own purposes. He has rushed special legislation through the State Senate, aimed directly at me. He formed an Emergency Charity Board, and through it confiscated my bank holdings while repressing all news of it.

"He ordered this home of mine condemned, and now his political machine owns it, though they allow me to remain here for appearance's sake. They haven't dared to crush me openly, but they've stripped me of my papers, my fortune, the men who once stood by me. That damnable despot has literally pilloried me, as he does every man who opposes him!"

"No one in the state is able to fight him?" Jimmy Christopher asked quickly.

"No one dares! He's more powerful than any king! There's no longer any such thing as freedom or justice in this state—there's only Young's tyranny. To oppose him is suicide!"

"Yet," Operator 5 insisted, "the people support him. His chances of being elected President of the United States are excellent."

"Most of the people support him because he's tricked them into believing he's a great man. By a few tax reductions, by creating useless jobs for the unemployed, by promising wealth to every man, by bribery and cajolery he gained the backing of

TIM DONOVAN

the people. The others support him because they fear to oppose him. Those who actually fight him are jailed on trumped-up charges—or they disappear—or they contract this damnable 'plague'!

"My boy, you must leave this house. Not only the house, but this state! It's hopeless trying to oppose Young. You're taking your life in your hands by—"

Operator 5 interrupted firmly, levelly. "Mr. Stockard, the

forces of Governor Young have now spread beyond the borders of this state. His power is a threat to the safety of the United States. I am a servant of my government, and I have sworn to do everything in my power to preserve it. I can let nothing stop me from fighting the danger Governor Young represents—nothing! I intend to see it through to the end."

"But you're almost alone in—"

"You have verified my suspicions, Mr. Stockard. Young's power is a blight threatening the existence of our government. The people do not realize the danger they face. I shall do my best to open their eyes... I came here with two missions. One of them is personal—it concerns a girl who is very dear to me, whom you must know. A reporter for the Amalgamated Press, Diane Elliot, who dared publish the truth about Young. You've heard of her?"

"Yes!" The emaciated man's eyes widened. "But I can tell you nothing of her—nothing except that she defied Governor Young and—disappeared. She may have paid for that with her life!"

Operator 5 straightened. In his mind he saw again the dark clearing in the woods, the black-uniformed firing-squad, the condemned prisoners—and among them a girl of Diane's age.

He heard again the clattering reports of the rifles, saw the dead bodies fall—among them a girl like Diane. A wretched chill came to his heart.

He bent forward to whisper. "Try to escape from this house and this state, Mr. Stockard. Your only hope of life is to—"

Stockard's parched lips trembled and his ghastly eyes stared past Operator 5.

"Look out!" he gasped. *"Behind you!"*

JIMMY CHRISTOPHER spun. The connecting door was opening. Through the widening crack the lean figure of Dr. Hurwit was visible. The physician's evil face was twisted into a grimace of hate; his one thin hand was gripping an automatic. The weapon was rising on a direct line with Jimmy Christopher's heart.

Swiftly Operator 5 stepped aside. As he moved he swung one arm to strike the shade of the standing-lamp. It crashed to the floor; the bulb splintered; darkness burst in the room. At the same instant a stab of flame cut the gloom. A deafening shock jarred the air, and a bullet spanged past his head.

Operator 5 sprang forward as a dry cry of terror broke from the lips of Stockard. He flung himself to the half-open door, drove a blow through it, full into the face of the physician. Blinded by the power of Jimmy Christopher's blow, Dr. Hurwit staggered, snarling with rage.

In the next room a dim light was burning; and into that room Operator 5 sprang. Dr. Hurwit, wheeling against the wall, jerked his automatic up.

Jimmy Christopher's hand flashed to the buckle of his belt.

A quick touch clicked it loose; he jerked the leather band free of its loops. It sprang out straight and true, baring the gleaming blade of a rapier. Operator 5's hand clenched about the hilt of the supple blade. He whipped it downward, and its steel clashed with the steel of Dr. Hurwit's gun.

The sharp edge slashed across the back of the physician's hand, and drew blood. The needle-point struck, paralyzed the doctor's trigger finger. A quick thrust, and the blade snatched at the automatic with the power of black magic. The heavy gun spun out of the physician's numbed hand.

A cry of rage broke from Dr. Hurwit's lips as Jimmy Christopher stepped forward—a cry that choked off as the stinging point of the *épée* touched, then poised upon the physician's constricted throat.

"My compliments, Doctor," Operator 5 said grimly, "to Governor Ursus Young!"

Suddenly a heavy pounding sounded on the front entrance of the house. Knuckles rapped sharply; husky voices demanded entrance. From the dry throat of William Stockard, in the next room, echoed a new cry of terror.

"The Cheka! The Cheka! They're here!"

Operator 5 stepped forward swiftly, drove a stiff-fingered blow to Dr. Hurwit's temple. A moan issued from the physician's lips; instantly he went rigid, and like an overbalanced statue toppled to the floor.

Jimmy Christopher whirled to the door. He knew his ju-jitsu blow would render Dr. Hurwit unconscious for at least an hour.

From the entrance came a renewed burst of pounding.

Past the terrified William Stockard, Jimmy Christopher sped. He clicked out the lights when he reached the rear entrance, and spun through. As he reached the rear steps, a black figure rushed at him—a uniformed corpsman. A gun glittered.

Operator 5's blade slashed at the hand gripping it; his fist drove out in a swift blow. It was not a ju-jitsu tactic which spilled the guard back into the grass, but a thoroughly American straight-arm jab. Jimmy leaped across the rolling body in the grass; and then he was a blurred ghost flitting across the grounds.

Whirling against the wall, he glimpsed shadowed figures rushing into the big gate, spreading to surround the house. The doctor had, as Stockard had warned, called the Blacks and the secret police—they were swarming into the estate. In the street, cars were flocking, bringing another squad. The whole mob of them—killers, predatory manhunters—were crowding with grim purpose into the grounds.

Operator 5's swift bound carried him over the ivy-covered wall. Again he crouched in deep shadow. A car carrying still another detail of Blacks whirred past as he stiffened in the concealment of a tree trunk. He leaped across the street, vaulted a fence, huddled again. From the gloom nearby, an anxious voice called.

"Jimmy! Jimmy!"

The tough Irish boy scurried to his side. Tim Donovan had worked hand and hand with Operator 5 on a number of highly important cases. He possessed unfailing courage, unbounded admiration for the Intelligence Operator whose unofficial assistant he was.

Again and again he had faced death at the side of Jimmy Christopher. Now they huddled together in the gloom, confronted by a danger exceeding any other in their experience—the legal power a political tyrant possessed to pronounce sentence of death on them without even a trial.

Operator 5 had said: "We are in as great danger here as if we were spies in enemy country in time of war!" and the full truth of that appalling statement now confronted them both.

"Steady, Tim!" cried Operator 5. "Take no chances! We're marked men! If the Blacks find us, we'll never be heard from again!"

CHAPTER 3
SUICIDE STRATAGEM

N O HINT of the terror ruling both city and state was evident in the brightly lighted business center of Hartland. The streets were crowded with automobiles—new, bright, powerful cars. The sidewalks were thronged with pedestrians who were well-dressed, who spent money lavishly. The shops were busy; laughter and good cheer prevailed. Visitors from out of the state, looking upon the scene, frequently remarked:

"This is prosperity returned! The depression no longer exists here. Governor Young has performed an economic miracle."

These visitors did not suspect that this was exactly what Governor Young wanted them to say. They did not dream that they were being deluded with a scene enacted for their benefit by thousands of Young's hirelings. They did not know that the cars, the clothing, the money were provided by the State Treasury, that the Treasury had acquired it by summarily confiscating wealth from hundreds of victims who had no redress. Visitors accepted Young Square as a true picture of prosperity when, in reality, it was a staged spectacle, false to its very center.

Behind a dozen show-spots in the city, all dressed in counterfeit colors upon orders of the Governor, the true conditions prevailed. Homes that were patrolled under false quarantine. Jails, crowded with respectable men and women, who had been imprisoned without trial, in filthy buildings, herded about like animals to be bought and sold—because they were opponents of the Governor. State Institutions packed with others who had dared voice opposition to the despotic Young.

Thousands being dealt scanty food supplies by ration cards— food which could be—and was—denied them at the whim of the dictator. Fear everywhere, liberties destroyed, businesses confiscated, homes endangered, with the ominous shadow of Governor Young blanketing away the principles of true American government.

Yet in Young Square the visitors said, "Governor Young is the man of the hour, the man who can lead us to new heights of prosperity, the man we need in the President's chair."

INTO THE false glitter of the square, a taxi crawled from a dark side street to discharge two passengers. Operator 5 and Tim Donovan hurried into the foyer of a tall building. A moment later, high above the street, they entered an office filled with clicking typewriters, clattering telegraph instruments.

This was the Hartland bureau of the Amalgamated News

Service, and Jimmy Christopher's card was a passport which opened the way for him straight to the desk of the wire chief.

The middle-aged chief, in shirt-sleeves, face colored by the green of his eye-shade, pushed aside a sheaf of copy and peered deeply into Jimmy Christopher's eyes. He glanced around warily, at an empty desk beside him. His manner was fearful, his eyes a warning.

"I want all the information you can give me," Operator 5 told him crisply, "concerning Diane Elliot."

The wire chief leaned forward suddenly. "For God's sake, don't mention her name! I can tell you nothing about her! I warned her not to write of Young as she did, but she went ahead anyway. No one can help her now!"

"She was working out of this bureau, and you were the last to see her," Operator 5 insisted. "Governor Young's Blacks are hunting for me—I can't stay here long. You must—"

"Listen!" The wire chief spoke in a sibilant whisper. "Our souls are not our own. We are not running a news service any longer. We've been forced into being propaganda spreaders for Young. We don't dare tell the truth. We say what Young wants us to say. If we didn't, we would—disappear, as Diane Elliot disappeared!"

"I insist upon knowing—"

There was the sound of a step behind the wire chief, and his eyes flashed a new warning. To the adjacent desk had come a man—a hard-faced, black-eyed person whose gaze searched that of Operator 5. Immediately the wire chief said, more loudly so that the newcomer would overhear:

"Certainly—we're in a better condition than any other state in the country. We're prosperous, thanks to Governor Young. He deserves to be elected President, and he will be."

Operator 5, taking the hint, asked about economic conditions in the state. As he talked and listened, he watched the other man. The wire chief, with apparent absentmindedness, scrawled on a sheet of copy paper while continuing to echo the praises of Governor Young. In a burst of simulated enthusiasm he leaned forward and held the sheet so that Jimmy Christopher could read:

> He's Young's man—censor—no word goes onto our wires without his approval—one word from him and I would be jailed and another Young man put in my place—be wise and forget about Diane Elliot.

Hastily the wire chief tore the sheet to bits, dropped them into a wastebasket.

Jimmy Christopher rose, his eyes shining darkly. "I will not forget—to vote for Governor Young," he said. "Goodnight."

Quickly, he left the office, the gaze of the dark-eyed man following him suspiciously. In the street, Operator 5 walked briskly, Tim at his side. He said nothing until they turned a quiet corner and were walking along a gloomy row of house fronts. Then he exclaimed, in cold amazement, "Young's power is everywhere, Tim! The country knows nothing of the true state of affairs here. And think of these conditions spread over the entire United States!"

Pausing at a doorway, he glanced back warily. Behind this

innocent looking house front, he knew, lay the offices occupied by Headquarters HNC of the United States Intelligence Service. It was connected with Central Headquarters WDC-13, in Washington, by secret telephone and teletype wires. It was the one agency he could turn to as a means of communicating with his Chief.

He closed his hand on the knob, was about to enter.

A QUICK, dark movement startled him.

From an adjoining doorway a young man lurched, face shaded by a low-pulled hat and a high-turned collar. The man staggered as if drunk, and the fumes of alcohol reached Operator 5's nostrils. The other stumbled against him, mumbled an apology, and staggered away.

At the first warning motion, Operator 5's hand had slipped to his armpit holster. He stood tight-nerved, until the young man, with a quick, swaying walk, passed from sight.

Operator 5 hesitated. His eyes became dark with thought. But he stepped across the sill with Tim.

They entered a dark vestibule. The gleam of a flashlight sprang out of the gloom, swept across their features. They stood motionless while being scrutinized.

Out of the emptiness behind the light a voice demanded:

"Password?"

"Freedom."

"Countersign?"

"Equality."

The light dropped, its glow disclosing the sharp face of the sentry, and Operator 5 and Tim Donovan were led back to a doorway. They passed through two empty rooms, climbed a flight of stairs, came at last to another door. Again passwords were exchanged. The guards opened the way to an office where a bright light hung low over a desk littered with communications. At the desk, working busily, sat a lean-faced man in shirtsleeves.

He came to his feet as Operator 5 asked: "You're V-4, the Hartland chief?"

"I am. You're Operator 5? We were advised by Z-7 that you were coming."

Jimmy Christopher studied the lean face of the man who had identified himself as V-4. He quickly noted a shiftiness of the other's eyes, a suggestion of cruelty in the line of the lips. An inner warning urged him to caution. He said, carefully:

"I have important details to report to Z-7. I should like a private telephone line at once."

He was conducted into an adjoining office: the Communications Room. A room pervaded by a strange quiet.

Usually, Operator 5 knew, the Communications Rooms of the scattered Intelligence Headquarters hummed with activity: teletypes chattering continually, men on duty at shortwave installations, telephones ringing a continual chorus. Here only one man was on duty, at the switchboard; here the unnatural quiet was ominous.

Operator 5 gave directions to the agent at the switchboard, then entered a booth. As he waited for his call to connect with the Washington Headquarters, his hand strayed into his coat pocket. He felt the crisp crackle of paper—and in surprise drew out a folded sheet. It was a closely written message he had never seen before. And as he read, cold dread filled him.

I am Operator K-2. Note the address below. This office is no longer Intelligence Headquarters. The man pretending to be the chief is not V-4. None of the men in the office are Intelligence agents. Two days ago HNC was raided by Young's Black Corps. V-4 was arrested and dragged away under Article 100. Every other operator was taken into custody. I am the only one who escaped. God knows what has happened to the rest.

Before the raid we received word that Operator 5 would report after smuggling himself into the state. I will wait for you and pass you this message. It is the only way I dare try to communicate with you. Young's secret police are trying to find me. I will be charged with treason, under Article 100, if I am caught—and the same fate will fall to you. There is no way of warning Washington over our wires. Young is now using HNC as his Headquarters for a branch of his secret police. The real HNC has been ruthlessly destroyed. Young has learned many vital secrets of the Intelligence, and he intends to make use of them against us. I warn you not to try to reach Washington and Z-7. Get out of this state at the soonest possible moment.

And beware of Young!

K-2.

THE CHILL tightened Operator 5's heart more and more as he read. And then the sudden jangle of the telephone startled him. He hesitated, removed the receiver, heard the man at the switchboard say: "WDC-13 on the wire, Z-7 speaking."

Cautiously Jimmy Christopher spoke. "Operator 5 reporting, Chief. Our suspicions are unfounded. Governor Young has regimented the state admirably and legally, and we owe him our support as the President-elect of the United States. He is held in the highest esteem here in Hartland. I suggest that I return to Washington at once, as there is no reason for my investigating conditions further."

The voice which answered over the wire was that of the man who controlled the destinies of the United States Intelligence over all the world—a man known, even to his most trusted agents, only as Z-7. "Are you quite sure of that, my boy?"

"Quite, Chief. I will write my report at once. File it under Twenty-three."

"I understand. Goodnight."

Operator 5 left the booth quickly. He saw the man at the switchboard tip a cam into neutral, and knew that the false V-4 had listened in on the conversation. His cheeks still prickled coldly as he returned to the center office, where Tim Donovan was waiting, unaware of the trap into which they had walked.

The false V-4 rose, with eyes blazing. "I took the liberty," he said huskily, "of assuring myself beyond all doubt that you are Operator 5—by listening in on your conversation with Z-7."

Quietly Jimmy Christopher answered: "I know that."

The man masquerading as V-4 stepped quickly to the door of the Communications Room, drew it shut, and locked it. At the door through which Operator 5 and Tim Donovan had entered he repeated the act. The third door, behind the desk, he left ajar. Then he drew open a drawer of his desk. Jimmy Christopher's darkening eyes followed every move, and Tim Donovan sensed the tightening of his nerves.

"It is no secret to me," the false V-4 said steadily, "that Signal Twenty-three means 'Disregard this entire report. It is totally false.'"

Operator 5 smiled slowly. He stepped toward one of the filing cabinets which completely walled the room. Consulting a chart marked with intricate cross-references, he rolled one of the drawers open, removed a folder. From it he lifted a photograph, to which typed sheets were clipped. He glanced through them quickly, and his smouldering gaze went to the face of the false V-4.

"When you searched these files and learned the secrets of the Intelligence Service," he said steadily, "you neglected to remove this information. It is no secret to me now that you are Clark Frey, once an international espionage agent, a man with a record in three United States prisons. Four years ago you were convicted of murder in the first degree here in Hartland, and since being pardoned by Governor Young you have been one of his chief spreaders of terrorism. For engineering the raid on this Headquarters, for the abduction of the real V-4 and his operators, you will one day pay the full penalty."

The eyes of the ex-convict Frey flashed coldly. Abruptly he stepped back, swung his hand up from the open drawer of the desk. Spinning to the door he had left ajar, he flung his arm forward. At the same instant that he hurled a glittering object across the room at Operator 5, he stepped across the sill, slapped the door shut, and shot a bolt into its socket.

A HOLLOW burst of sound filled the office as the spherical glass bomb exploded. The thing whizzed over Jimmy Christopher's shoulder, as he swiftly sidestepped, and shattered upon the front of a cabinet. Instantly white fumes swelled into the air, clouding like thick fog under the light.

As swiftly, Jimmy Christopher darted across the room, grasped the arm of Tim Donovan, pulled the boy to his side.

"Jimmy! What is it?"

Quickly Operator 5 slipped a small metal case from his vest pocket, clicked it open. From it he removed two pairs of white, oval wafers—wafers of unglazed porcelain, impregnated with a preparation he had compounded in his New York workshop. In the past they had stood him in good stead; he was never without them. Now he passed a pair to the Irish lad.

"Quick, Tim! That gas is cacodyl isocyanide—one breath will kill you! The filters will neutralize it. Hurry!" In the same moment he slipped his own pair deftly into his nostrils.

The dismayed boy swiftly slipped the porcelain filters in place, and, motionless, they stood side by side while the white fog drifted across the room, dimming the lights, bringing a sharp sting to their eyes.

Operator 5 slipped his automatic into his hand as he signaled caution to the boy. Leaning close, he whispered: "Don't make the slightest sound. Frey must believe the gas has killed us. He has armed men all through the building. Our only hope of getting out is—"

He broke off as a step sounded outside the door through which Frey had escaped. Silence followed that single step.

Jimmy Christopher crossed the room noiselessly. There was no window in any wall; the doors were the only possible means of exit. Quietly he unscrewed one of the two bulbs of the light fixture hanging low above the desk. He drew his automatic and inserted the barrel into the emptied socket. A spark flashed: instantly the room as dark. The short circuit had blown a fuse in the main line.

Operator 5 drifted from the desk, seized Tim Donovan's arm, drew him close to the door through which they had entered. Pressed against the wall, gun leveled, he waited.

The step from outside sounded again. The bolt clicked. Then the knob turned.

As the door inched open, faint light streamed in from beyond, blending through the lethal fog. In the glow a man appeared—a man whose head was enclosed in a long-snouted gas mask, whose goggled eyes peered into the mist, whose hand gripped a huge automatic. Muttering through the rubberized fabric, peering at the floor, he stepped all the way inside.

Operator 5, muscles tense as springs, slid across the sill, drawing Tim Donovan after him. Hearing another step, he whirled. In the glow of the hallway a second gas-masked figure hurried forward, peering through his grotesque lenses. In sheer amazement he stared at the two who stepped, alive and without masks, from the clouds of death-dealing fog.

That instant's hesitation was enough for Operator 5. Swiftly he drove a blow past the tube of the second man's aspirator—a blow which struck hard above the heart. A hissing gasp sounded inside the mask. Its wearer staggered against the wall, and Jimmy Christopher followed his blow with a second. A ju-jitsu attack crashed his assailant all the way downward, and he whirled back at once, toward the door. The other gas-masked man was already groping out through the fog.

Operator 5 slammed the door shut, shot the bolt into its socket, whirled away as knuckles pounded the panels and a muffled voice roared: "Open the door! Let me out! This mask is leaking!" Jimmy Christopher exclaimed: "Fast, Tim!" and sped down the stairs. He whirled into the lower hall just as two shadowy figures sped from the entrance.

OPERATOR 5'S automatic blazed swiftly three times. Then he swung from the base of the stairs, Tim Donovan darting along at his side.

The slap of an opening door sounding from the rear of the hall caused the boy to whirl. A dark-faced man sprang into the hall—a man clad in the dread black uniform of the Young Corpsmen. He swung his rifle to his shoulder, took swift aim squarely at the back of Jimmy Christopher.

Tim Donovan leaped with the fury of a wild animal. He gripped the barrel of the rifle and tipped it downward. It spat a slug into the floor as the corpsman struck a savage blow, and the tough little Irish lad flung himself into a kicking, clawing, biting battle. With all the strength of his compact body he fought the killer, who was thrice his weight. His savage attack threw the uniformed man off balance, and they sprawled in wild combat on the floor.

Jimmy Christopher slid swiftly along the wall, even while the sound of Tim's frantic struggle came from behind him. The two armed guards were screened by baffling gloom. A faint twinkle of light on gunmetal drew a bullet from Operator 5's automatic with lightning swiftness. A howl of pain answered; a gun thumped to the floor. Jimmy Christopher swung toward the entrance and glanced back in time to see Tim Donovan scrambling up from the dazed corpsman.

A bullet crashed out of the darkness and its hot breath blasted against Operator 5's neck. So swiftly that the two reports blended into one, he answered the shot. Fingernails scratched the wall as the man he had hit clawed for support.

Operator 5 backed to the entrance and Tim Donovan sprang panting to his side. One swift movement took them outside.

"Stick close, Tim!"

They raced to the gloomy corner, sidled into a doorway as they glimpsed black-clad figures ahead. At the next intersection two uniformed corpsmen were on duty. Jimmy Christopher glanced along each angle of the crossing streets, and in each of the four directions he saw men in black uniforms who would shoot quickly, to kill, if he and Tim attempted to break past an alarm. He heard, from the house that had once been Headquarters HNC, the slam of the door. Men came running out.

With desperate swiftness he darted to the center of the street.

52

Stooping to fasten his fingers in the holes of a circular metal plate bearing the marks of the municipal telephone company, he commanded Tim quickly, and swung the cover away.

Breathlessly the boy scrambled down. Operator 5 dropped through, spread his legs, braced them against the lead-covered trunk lines conduited below. He slipped the cover-plate back, and dropped into utter darkness.

In the damp, black, muffled space they huddled, shivering as they listened to the rumbling noises above, on the street. The cover clinked as one of the searching secret police of Governor Young ran past overhead. Then, except for the slow drip of water, there was silence.

CHAPTER 4
DEFIANCE TO TERROR

AT THE border of a spreading park, topped by a golden dome, sat the impressive white stone capitol of New Cornwall. Above its broad steps Corinthian pillars rose to support chaste marble on which the motto of the great State— *Liberty—Equality—Justice*—was engraved. Beyond that motto, in that building, lay the Headquarters of terror, the domain of the god of the dictatorship—the offices of Governor Ursus Young.

Black-uniformed corpsmen patrolled the steps. Others of the dread soldiers of fear stood at attention in the marble hallways. The smaller offices, devoted to the administrative and judicial departments of the state, were occupied by the patron puppets of Young. In the far wing of the great building, guarded by a detachment of his battalions of terror, were the most sumptuous offices of all, occupied by Young himself.

Tonight, with only hours to wait until his name would be voted upon from coast to coast as a candidate for the Presidency of the United States—voted upon and, he felt confident, chosen—Governor Young sat at his massive desk.

He was a huge man, with close-cropped iron-gray hair, and a ruddy, hard face apparently molded of clay and baked in a kiln. He did not glance—he peered. His bearing was that of a feudal baron. There was power in his presence; yet it was a power of evil, a force which achieved its ends by threats, intimidation, cajolery, by discriminating bribery and fear. His merciless drive, his heartless cruelty, his indomitable will had made him a demagogic political wizard whose equal did not exist in American history.

Beside his desk stood an officer of the Black Troops, at stiff attention. He had brought to Young a document, for signature—one of a score that officer had seen signed at that desk. The phrases of the document spelled doom. "By virtue of the power… under Article One Hundred… prisoners of the State… penalty of death… the high crime of Treason…." To it, Governor Ursus Young affixed his signature without even glancing at the names of those he was condemning to die.

The Black Officer took the document, saluted, strode out the door—taking the first steps on a mission which would not end until the doomed were dead by the rifles of a firing squad and buried in an unmarked grave in the woods under the dark of night.

A buzzer sounded. Governor Young heard—but four other men in the office did not. Men even more massive than Young, they were standing at the four walls. Holstered forty-fives bulged their coats. Their faces were cruelly blank. They were the body-guards of the governor—men never out of sight of him, never more than an arm-length away when he moved in the open. They would kill at his gesture. He had chosen them to stand at his side night and day because they could neither hear nor repeat anything said in their presence. They were deaf-mutes.

Young's pressure on a button brought an excited, middle-aged man into the office. The face of this man, who was Young's secretary, was flaccid with the smug stupidity of a small-time politician whose only office was to obey the commands of his boss.

He thrust a bit of paper before Young's hard eyes and exclaimed:

"He's outside now—waiting!"

Young's dark brows lowered. His face twisted with both surprise and rage. The message was one he had never expected to see. It read:

> I request a brief audience.
>
> Operator 5, USI.

"God's sake!" blurted Melvard Gorad, Young's secretary. "All the secret police in the city looking for him, and he turns up here! Say the word, and—"

"Show him in," Young commanded.

Gorad swallowed. "What?"

The Governor's thick lips curled craftily. "He's dangerous.

He's the most dangerous man in the country. He's got a good reason for deliberately coming here. I can handle him. Show him in."

The amazed Secretary hurried out. In a moment the door opened again. Operator 5, his manner brisk, advanced to the desk. He did not offer his hand; nor did Governor Young. They scrutinized each other during a moment of silence, while the four deaf-mutes watched warily.

The Governor said casually, "I have heard of you, young man. You are the most valuable member of the United States Intelligence Service. I will be proud to have you under my command when I become President."

Jimmy Christopher said wryly: "Thank you."

"You are here on some special case?"

"I am here to locate a girl who is very dear to me—an unofficial member of the Intelligence. She disappeared mysteriously after printing an attack upon you, Governor Young."

Young's face darkened. "I know the facts in that case. You can put it down to an underhanded trick of my enemies, an attempt to discredit me. The girl was kidnapped, and filthy rumors are placing the blame on me. That's the object of it—a political trick on the eve of election. I have done and am doing everything possible to find the guilty parties."

Jimmy Christopher's lips twisted sourly. "You need not continue the effort, Governor. I have located her."

"You've what—?" Young broke off sharply. "I congratulate you! But how—?"

"I know where she is being kept, and I aim going to release

her at once. I have come here to inform you that those responsible for her disappearance will be punished for the crime regardless of their position or political prominence."

Young feigned indignity. "Is it possible you believe the baseless charges made against me—that I had a hand in it? Allow me to assure you that if any of my men are responsible, unknown to me, I will punish them myself—and to the limit! I want the truth to be known!"

"The truth, Governor," Jimmy Christopher declared levelly, "*will* be known." He stepped forward briskly. "I have my own men. I wish no help from any of your agencies, beyond orders to your frontier sentries—who are there, of course, only because of the epidemic—that my companions and I will be allowed to pass out of the state unhindered. Will you assure me that this will be done?"

"You have my word of honor!" Young boomed. "I will guarantee you every protection and convenience!"

Operator 5 bowed. "Thank you. I expect to take Miss Elliot out of the state before dawn. Goodnight!" Turning briskly on his heel, he strode out the door.

When it closed, Governor Young stared at it for an instant, his eyes glinting with repressed rage. Then his hand shot out to the inter-office telephone on the desk. He leaned forward when a gruff voice rasped from it: "Orders, Governor?"

"Operator 5 is now leaving the State House. He declares that he knows where the girl reporter is being held. Capture him! Do it carefully—be certain he has none of his men with him and that there are no witnesses—but capture him! Torture him, if necessary, to find out exactly how much he knows. If he knows too much—!" Young broke off ominously. "Also double the guard on that girl! Those are your orders!"

"We'll handle him!"

Governor Young's eyes turned again to the door through which Operator 5 had stepped. And now his eyes, which had glittered with icy hatred, gleamed as well with grim triumph. As a political tactician he was as cruel, as wily as a stalking fox— yet he did not dream that, when issuing his orders of doom, he had fallen into a trap neatly prepared for him by Operator 5....

JIMMY CHRISTOPHER ran smartly down the broad steps of the State House. Tim Donovan hurried to his side as he strode out of the area of light given off from the great golden dome. He glanced back once and saw two black-clad men hurry from the great building, into the shadows, where they melted from sight as they began to trail him. In a grimly jubilant whisper he declared to Tim Donovan:

"It's working, old-timer!"

"Jimmy, what have you done?" The boy looked anxious.

"I've deliberately made myself an open target for Governor Young. I've deliberately led him to believe that I know where Diane Elliot is—in hopes that he'll *betray* her hiding place. It's our only chance—our only possible chance of locating her, old-timer. It may bring me a bullet in the back, but—"

"Jimmy! Isn't there any other way?"

"Not with our Headquarters destroyed, not while Young's secret police are stalking us. Walk fast, Tim! There's a car following—the Blacks are trailing us!"

He turned into a dark street. Gloomy and deserted along its entire length, it was a deliberate invitation to attack. Operator 5 strode briskly, without glancing back. But with a quickening pulse he sensed that the car carrying the Black Corpsmen was drawing nearer. He walked more rapidly, into a still darker region, while the car crept up behind. Suddenly it spurted ahead, swung into the curb.

"Steady, Tim! We've got to take those men!"

Two black-uniformed troopers stepped from the car and planted themselves in Jimmy Christopher's path. When he paused, they peered at him stonily. Their fingers curled around the butts of their guns.

One of them demanded gruffly: "Where's your Health Certificate?"

Operator 5 promptly answered: "Right here."

His hand rose as though to slip inside his coat—and flashed so swiftly it became a blur. With the speed of light he struck, driving stiff fingers to the center of the one corpsman's forehead, even while flinging his other hand upward. A hoarse cry broke from the lips of the second trooper as the attacking fingers clamped to his throat. The first stiffened with a quick exhalation of breath, the second recoiled from the force of Operator 5's onslaught.

"Get him out of sight, Tim!"

Jimmy Christopher's fingers pressed deep in the throat of the second trooper, and felt a nerve click there. The man's big black-gloved hand, jerking a gun upward, stopped as if petrified. Operator 5 snatched the gun away, whirled to see Tim

Donovan dragging the other burly corpsman into the shadow of a stoop. Both men had gone rigid, paralyzed instantly by the deft ju-jitsu blows.

Operator 5 pulled his own victim close to the one Tim had dragged. He glanced back and forth alertly along the gloomy street. No pedestrians were in sight; there was no sound save the clicking of the idling motor. Operator 5 bounded up the stoop to the door of the tenement. He listened, peering through grimy glass, then brought out his pack of master-keys.

The lock, a simple type, yielded at once to the implement—which could have opened far more intricate mechanisms. Quickly Jimmy Christopher carried his man into the dark hall-way. Tim Donovan left the second lying in the shadow. They closed the door, listened again, waited.

"Be very quiet, Tim!" Operator 5 whispered. "There are people asleep in this house. Watch the street!"

THE BOY stood guard at the door, his heart pounding. First, stealthy sounds came from the darkness behind him. Then silence. Long moments passed. At last footfalls came toward him and he looked around. A gasp of amazement passed his lips. Operator 5 had come to his side garbed in the black uniform of the terror troopers!

"All quiet, Tim?"

"Sure, Jimmy! Gee! What're you going to do?"

Operator 5 came back with a rush; his knuckled hand shot
across the desk to the police chief's head!

"You'll see, old-timer."

They returned to the rear of the hallway, where the unconscious trooper lay stripped. Lifting him together, they carried him through the door of a closet. Operator 5 removed, from the pocket of his civilian coat, two small coils of stout silken string, bound the unconscious corpsman's hands and ankles. He tied a handkerchief gag in place. Then, folding his civilian clothing, he placed it inside a paper box he had noticed in the closet, and handed it to the boy.

"Hold the light, Tim!"

In the glow he examined the contents of the uniform pockets. A wallet card identified the unconscious man as Arto Elias, Corporal of the Special State Guard. The card bore the flourishing signature of Governor Young. The rest of the things in the man's pockets were odds and ends.

Operator 5 tried the knob of a door across the hall, and found the way locked. Again he brought his master-keys into use, then swung the beam of his light into a shabby living room. Closed doors shut off a bedroom beyond. Quietly he entered, opened drawers, found writing-paper and pen. While Tim Donovan held the torch he wrote carefully, painstakingly, studying each stroke as he made it.

He got up at last, folded the sheet, stuffed it inside his tunic. He returned to the front entrance. Beside the stoop, in deep shadows, the second of the unconscious troopers still lay. Operator 5, signaling Tim Donovan to his side, strode past, to the car at the curb.

"In the back seat, Tim—and keep out of sight!" he ordered.

"My plan is all set. Watch sharp—and remember, if anything happens to me, you're to slip out of the state and report to Z-7 at all costs!"

The wide-eyed boy ducked into the darkness below the rear seat of the Black Trooper car. Jimmy Christopher took the wheel, started the car, swung it roundabout, and brought it to a stop facing in the opposite direction, closer to the unconscious man. He slipped out, knelt above the corpsman. Probing a major nerve in the neck, he manipulated swiftly. Returning consciousness stirred the trooper.

"What happened?" he muttered.

Jimmy Christopher seized his shoulders, shook him. "Wake up! What's the matter?"

The dazed man straightened, peering into Jimmy Christopher's face. The visor of the helmet shaded it; the high, black collar gave it a squarer aspect. Operator 5 dragged his man up from the shadow and flashed the light into his eyes.

"Where—where are they?" the fellow blurted breathlessly. "They've got away! We had 'em and—where's Elias? God, the Governor'll—"

"Who got away?" Operator 5 demanded. "Say, I saw a young guy and a kid beating it around the corner just before I spotted you lying here. I heard him say, 'We've got twenty men…. We'll get the girl right away.' They beat it out of sight and—"

"God!" the other burst out. "Twenty men! There ain't that many around the girl this time of night—they'll get her if we don't warn 'em! Where's my car? How—"

"Get into mine," Operator 5 commanded. "I'll take you to

the girl right away. Make it snappy, brother! If anything's gone wrong—you know what the Governor'll do about it!"

IN TERROR, the trooper ducked into the car at the curb. Jimmy Christopher slipped behind the wheel. The dash-lights were off; no gleam shone in his face. The other, breathing quickly, gave desperate orders: "Quick—Police Headquarters!" Operator 5's eyes darkened. "Okay! Is she there? I'll go by Young Street and—"

"No—straight ahead! It's shorter!"

Grimly Operator 5 sent the car whirring along the street. Behind him, in the darkness, he knew Tim Donovan was crouching.

Intersections flashed past. "Step on it—only a few blocks now!" the other man exclaimed frantically. Jimmy Christopher increased speed, gazing at a turreted building on a corner several squares ahead. He swung into the side street, brought the car to the curb, asked quickly:

"Are you sure she's in there—hasn't been moved?"

"I ought to know she's there! I took here there myself! God, if—"

Operator 5's one hand snatched at the trooper's shoulder. His other, stiff-fingered, clicked again to the other man's temple. Hot breath burst in his face; an expression of astonishment became a frozen mask on the face of the corpsman as swift paralysis sat him rigid in his seat.

Grimly Operator 5 allowed him to remain braced against the door, and slipped out. "Stay here, Tim!" he whispered.

"Diane's inside! Remember—we've got to get her clear, at all costs!"

He strode briskly to the entrance of the Police Headquarters building. The black uniform fitted him loosely, but, wearing it as though it were his accustomed garb, he made a smart figure.

Down a brick corridor he strode, reading the lettering on each door as he passed, turning to the one labeled *Chief of Police*. He knocked and, when a gruff voice growled, he entered.

To the florid-faced, surly mannered individual at the desk he proffered a paper drawn from his tunic. The chief—another tool of Governor Young—blinked at the message:

> The prisoner of the State, Diane Elliot, is to be placed in the custody of Corporal Elias at once, who is charged with transferring her to the State Asylum for the Insane. Carry out these orders without question.
>
> Ursus Young, Governor.

With cold dread in his heart, Operator 5 watched as the chief studied the forged signature. The beefy hand dragged a telephone close; the growling voice commanded: "Bring the Elliot girl to my office—right away." Jimmy Christopher repressed a grim smile as the chief sat back.

"I don't need no written orders from the Governor," the man declared. "All he has to do is telephone me when he wants anything done. He gave me this job, and I'm runnin' it the way he says."

Operator 5 waited anxiously until heels beat in the corridor. The door swung wide. Two men stepped in—men in the uniforms of policemen, but marionettes of the Governor. Between them they held the arms of a girl. Jimmy Christopher stepped back against the wall so that she would not see him at once.

Her clothing and hair were disarranged, her face was marked with heavy fatigue and despair, her lips were pale with fear. But her eyes had remained bright and defiant.

This was the girl whom Operator 5 had met at the height of a dangerous spy case, the girl who had helped him courageously in several dangerous situations, whose remarkable ability had won her an enviable position in the newspaper world. She alone, of hundreds of reporters in New Cornwall, had dared tell the truth about the despotic Governor—and now she gazed with open hostility at the official who was a mere dummy to do Young's bidding.

"That's all," the chief growled at the two men who had brought her in. And to the girl, as the pair withdrew: "You're goin' to a place, young woman, that you're never comin' out of."

HER EYES turned to the young man in black uniform. Instantly the name of Jimmy Christopher crowded joyously to her lips. But the warning glitter of his eyes silenced her at once. Quick-witted, alert, she immediately caught the significance of Operator 5's uniform; immediately realized the danger confronting him. Her stare became hostile as he stepped forward.

"Come along," he commanded. "You're going with me."

The chief's telephone rang. Jimmy Christopher took Diane's arm, had already turned her to the door when the chief's voice, speaking into the transmitter, stopped him.

"Sure, Governor! The girl?" His breath coming hotly, Operator 5 glanced into the corridor, seeing that it was empty. Diane's terrified eyes sought his as the voice of the chief boomed.

"Give her more guards? Wait a minute! There's somethin' wrong! I just got written orders from you to turn her over—I tell you—you didn't?" The chief was glaring at Jimmy Christopher. "Come back here, Corporal! Bring that girl back here and—"

Operator 5 came back—with a rush. His hard-knuckled fist shot across the desk, smashed to the beefy man's chin as the chief rose. The telephone clattered down, and the chief staggered back, clawing at the gun in his holster. Swiftly Jimmy Christopher rounded the desk, driving out two more hard blows. They crashed to the jaw of the big man, and he lurched against the wall, then slid down, unconscious.

"With me, Diane! Quick!"

Operator 5 whirled back to the door, stepped into the corridor with the breathless girl. As he strode to the entrance he heard quick steps. Turning, he saw a uniformed man hurry out from one door and across to the chief's. As he stepped into the street with the girl, a bellow of wrath echoed down the corridor.

"Stop that Corporal! Bring that girl back!"

Operator 5 thrust Diane into a run along the side of the building. Once near the car he exclaimed: "Get behind the building, Di—into the alley—quick!"

As the girl sped on, he spun to the waiting car. "Out, Tim! Follow Di! Wait!"

The tough little Irish lad sprang out of the darkness of the rear seat, gripping the box, and Operator 5 slipped under the wheel.

Tim Donovan sped toward the gloom of the alley, and Jimmy Christopher threw the car into gear. Already, men were crowding out of the Headquarters entrance—men on the run, gripping guns.

He thrust the hand-throttle open, released the clutch. The car spurted ahead as he carefully adjusted the wheel. He slipped out, slamming the door shut. The car whirred along the curb, gathering speed—a car carrying only an unconscious trooper. HALF A score of men came mobbing around the corner as Operator 5 jerked up his corpsman's heavy revolver. "There they go! After 'em!" He fired twice, swiftly, at the back of the car careening down the street.

As the grim men loosed a fusillade of lead at the streaking car, Operator 5 sprang back into the shadows. Shouldering against the building, he saw men scattering to other automobiles at the curb. Some leveled revolvers and drove slug after slug into the empty, plunging car.

Quickly Jimmy Christopher eased past the rear corner, into the gloom of the alley.

"Jimmy!" Diane Elliot's hot hand seized his as he whirled to Tim Donovan's side. Crouched out of sight, he saw half a dozen cars, carrying policemen, speeding after the one which was driverless! Roaring shots continued to ring from the street. A score of men rushed into the chase while Jimmy Christopher watched grimly.

"Jimmy!" Diane Elliot exclaimed again; and suddenly, impulsively, threw her arms around him. "Oh, Jimmy, I'm so glad to see you—so glad! I thought I'd never—never—" She pressed her hot lips to his, and her tears wet his cheek as she clung to him.

"Lord, Di—I thought I'd never find you! Good girl! We're not clear yet. We've got to get out of this state tonight if it's humanly possible—otherwise the Blacks will trap us and we'll disappear off the face of the earth. Our only chance—listen, wait here!"

Jimmy Christopher hurried deeper into the bleak alley, while the dismayed girl and the anxious boy gazed after him. He disappeared from their sight, and with dread weighting their hearts, they waited in the gloom.

Somewhere beyond, the cars of the police were speeding, shots were rocketing through the night. Suddenly lights gleamed along the alleyway and another car sped toward them. They recoiled in terror as it swung close and stopped.

"In—quick!"

The voice was Jimmy Christopher's. He had taken a car standing in front of Headquarters; had quickly manipulated the ignition-wiring so that he was able to start it. Now, at the wheel—a black-uniformed figure who would pass any casual scrutiny—he commanded the girl and the boy breathlessly. "Keep out of sight in the back seat—and pray!"

Into the street he swung the car again, while Diane and Tim huddled in the shadow behind him. Hands gripping the wheel, eyes alert, heart pounding, he sought his way across the city. At every corner danger lurked; every turn of the wheels was a risk. All the Black Corpsmen, all the dread secret police, he knew, were at this moment scouring the city for the escaped girl and for the despot Young's deadliest enemy—Operator 5.

CHAPTER 5
THE LURKING CHEKA

A T THE edge of Hartland, almost lightless, lay Cornwall Field, the U.S. Army post and Air Corps base. A beacon winked overhead; a few windows glowed; a sentry patrolled at the gate. In his quarters adjoining the Operations Offices, Major Anthony Taynor, Commanding Officer, had been uneasily asleep—until the jangling of the telephone bell aroused him. What be heard then filled him with amazement.

"Refer to Orders Thirty, Paragraph Four," a crisp voice over the line informed him. "At once! Emergency!"

The connection broke. In wrinkled pajamas, Major Taynor charged into his office, consulted strange orders he had received several days ago from the War Department and had kept under lock and key, carefully guarded, ever since. They were Orders Thirty. Paragraph Four read:

"Prepare one of your fastest pursuit planes, with sufficient fuel for a non-stop flight to Washington, D.C., and keep the preparations strictly secret."

Major Taynor's snapping orders had brought officers and ground crew hastening from their barracks. A plane had been wheeled from its hangar and fueled to the cap. It had been cranked into action. Now, it sat on the line, watched by wary men, its prop idling over.

Hastily dressed, the major stood watching the gate until headlights gleamed through it, and a car swung close to the plane.

He peered in amazement at the young man who slipped from the wheel—a young man wearing the uniform of a Corporal of the Black Troops. Operator 5 stepped close, glanced searchingly into the faces of the men around the plane. He crisply asked:

"From whom do you take orders, Major?"

Major Taynor's jaw-muscles bunched. "I take my orders from the General Staff and the Commander-in-Chief of the Army and Navy. If you are here to intimidate me into taking orders from Governor Young, you're wasting your time!"

Jimmy Christopher smiled. He slipped his thin silver case from inside his tunic, pressed the concealed spring and held before the widening eyes of the major the credentials signed by the President of the United States. Taynor's hand shot out.

"By God, sir, I'm glad to see you! I am at your service! Your plane is ready!"

Operator 5 shook the major's hand, then opened the rear door of the car. Tim Donovan and Diane Elliot slipped out, came to his side. He glanced around again and asked:

"I want your best pilot—is he here? Have you complete trust in these men?"

"Lieutenant Winfield will fly you to your destination, sir. These men are trustworthy, yes—but I warn you, there are spies on the post working for Governor Young. You'll have to take off at once unless you wish to run the danger of being stopped by Young's air patrol. There's not a moment to lose."

"I must take time to use your wireless equipment to communicate with my Headquarters in Washington, Major," Operator 5 insisted.

Major Taynor's face reddened. "Our wireless equipment," he declared, "is out of order. Sabotage, sir! The work of some of Young's spies—I'm sure of that. We've been unable to make repairs." The major stepped closer and spoke in a terse whisper.

"For God's sake, inform the War Department that I must have reinforcements! My men have been disappearing off this field. They take leave—and never come back. Two of my planes have vanished out of the sky. Three mysterious fires have broken out—fires intended to wipe this field out of existence. We are handicapped, crippled, virtual prisoners here because to venture out is to risk—disappearing. For God's sake get off this field and on your way at once!"

Again Jimmy Christopher's hand seized the major's. "I'll do everything possible to help remove the danger threatening you. Thank you for your assistance. We'll take off now."

QUICKLY HE helped Diane Elliot and Tim Donovan into the plane, then crawled into the rear cubby with them as Lieutenant Winfield took the controls. Grave-faced men watched as the radial roared; Major Taynor signaled good-luck anxiously. The brakes went free, the plane rolled, speeded, slashed into the air.

In the tearing wind, huddled beside the other two in the pit, Operator 5 looked down at the field as they roared away in the darkness. Quickly he snapped the switch of the shortwave installation; affixed a helmet containing earphones, brought a microphone to his lips. Carefully trimming the oscillator, he switched a distorter into the circuit. When he spoke he was flying high through the night sky, and his voice sped far ahead of him.

"Calling WDC-13. Operator 5 calling WDC-13 and Z-7!"

Almost at once, through a crackle of background static, a voice responded. "WDC-13—all clear. Z-7 is coming to the mike. One moment! Here he is!" The throaty, deep voice of the Washington Chief followed. "Listening, Operator 5!"

"I have just taken off Cornwall Field, Hartland, bound for Washington, Chief. Diane and Tim are with me. We're safe, but—"

"My boy, wait!" Z-7's voice crackled. "Thank God you've reached me at last. I am prepared for an appalling report—but before you make it, I must give you new orders, orders of the greatest urgency. You are not to return to Washington. You are to remain in Hartland!"

"What!" Operator 5's amazed exclamation crackled over the ether. "Certainly, Chief. To remain will be highly dangerous, but if you order it—"

"I order it," the voice of the Washington Chief declared quickly, "because a matter of the highest importance has come up. The President of the United States is about to leave Washington for New Cornwall. He is going to speak in Hartland tomorrow night."

"The President—coming here?" Operator 5 echoed the information in dismay as the plane weaved through the darkness. "Chief, he must not come! Even the President cannot escape the danger here! He must not run the risk!"

Z-7 retorted: "He has determined upon it, my boy. We have

all tried to dissuade him, but he will not alter his decision. He has decided to make the last speech in his campaign for reelection in Hartland, because it is the center of Young's power. It's a daring move, highly dangerous I know, but—he's coming, and you must remain, my boy, to warn him of the true conditions there, also to command his bodyguards so that he's protected at all costs."

Operator 5 paused, his eyes darkening with anxiety. "Chief, please switch your receiver into the telephone system. Connect me with the President at the White House at once. I must speak to him personally."

"Hold it. We'll have the connection in a moment."

Jimmy Christopher waited anxiously as his plane shuttled under the stars. He looked down into deep darkness. Hartland was left behind; it was a mere shining spot near the horizon. The powerful radial motor was ripping the plane through the sky at a dizzy speed. In a few moments the state border would pass beneath the wings—a border beyond which lay safety—safety from Young's murderous battalions of Blacks and secret police.

As the plane roared on, a new voice came over the ether.

It was grave, calm, confident. It was the voice of the President of the United States. Seated in his historic study in the White House, the Chief Executive of the nation spoke to Operator 5 in the plane speeding through the gloom of a coming dawn, hundreds of miles away.

"MY BOY, I'm delighted to hear your voice and to know that you are safe. You wish—"

"I wish to urge you not to come to Hartland, Mr. President,"

Operator 5 declared. "Even you are unaware of the frightfully dangerous situation here. To come will be to run the gravest possible risk. You must not take the chance of—"

"My boy," the President interrupted, "tomorrow night marks the crucial hours of the national campaign. I am determined to attack Governor Young's policies on his own grounds. It is not merely that I desire to be reelected. I am unalterably opposed to all that Governor Young stands for, and I have sworn to preserve the Constitution of the United States. It is my duty to fight Young to the limit of my ability, and I can do that only by attacking his regime in the very center of his armed camp."

"Mr. President," Operator 5 answered, "no one appreciates more than I do your courage and your high ideals. I admire you strongly for your decision. Yet I must insist—"

"I have, so far," the President continued, "been unable to reach past the borders of New Cornwall. Young has kept my previous speeches out of his press. He has refused to allow my coast-to-coast broadcasts to issue from any station within New Cornwall. He has done his utmost to eliminate me from the minds of the people of the state. To them there is only one candidate for the Presidency—Young. When I speak tomorrow night in Hartland, they will be forced to listen to me. I must do it!"

"Mr. President!" Operator 5's voice rang. "Again I insist—"

"You have served your country signally in the past, my boy," the grave voice of the President interrupted, "and I esteem you as a personal friend. But I must remind you that you are under my orders, and that my decision stands. I have already announced to the press that I will speak in Hartland tomorrow night—and I will, at the scheduled moment."

Operator 5 felt his face flush at the rebuke. "I beg your pardon, Mr. President. Only my anxiety for you prompted me to insist. Since you are determined to come, I will remain in Hartland—at your side."

"Very well. Goodnight, my boy!"

The telephonic connection broke. The voice of Z-7 sounded again over the ether. "Take care of yourself, Operator 5, and report to me at the soonest possible moment."

"I'll do my best, Chief!"

Jimmy Christopher straightened in the pit, while Diane Elliot and Tim Donovan studied his grave face. He reached over, slapped the back of his pilot. To the astounded Lt. Winfield he commanded:

"Turn back! To the Hartland field!"

Grimly his hands tightened on the cowling as the pilot swung the swift plane through a steep bank. When the crate leveled, its nose was pointing again in the direction of Young's stronghold of terror.

Operator 5 searched the sky, alert for the appearance of any of Young's aerial patrol; he peered ahead as the lights of Hartland swam up from the horizon. At top speed he was being carried back into the vortex of danger.

THE PLANE circled over the broad expanse of Cornwall Field, and Jimmy Christopher looked down. He noted lights moving on the tarmac—lights in pairs—the headlamps of automobiles. His nerves tightened when he caught a sparkling of fire—flashes like the exploding of guns on the dark field. The beams of the car headlights showed prostrate bodies on the sand. And suddenly, from the corner of the row of hangars, a brighter flare shone—naked flame!

"Down!" Jimmy Christopher commanded his pilot imperatively. "Full power!"

The swift plane soughed into the lower air with radial roaring, as Operator 5 continued to watch the amazing scene below.

Brighter each moment, the fire swept into the open hangars, surging on the wind, sending billowing clouds of oily smoke upward. Cars were swinging toward the gate. While the plane rocked down, the cars flocked outward, swerving into the road, scattering. But the darkness of the field was wiped away now by the fluttering flare of the hangar fire.

Jimmy Christopher's command sent his plane swooping to the ground at the far edge of the field. It touched three points, drove swiftly over smooth sand. Two cars, turning near the gate, paused as the roar of the radial carried across the field. Again spots of fire flashed—and slugs screamed into the slipstream of the pursuit. Jimmy Christopher's sharp command forced Diane and Tim low in the pit. He snapped his automatic into his hand as the two cars darted fleetingly past the gate.

Hard-pressed brakes stopped the plane. Operator 5 leaped down and stared coldly at an appalling picture.

The fire, whipped by the wind, was sweeping rapidly across the hangars. It was a certainty that they were doomed. In the glare of the flames, uniformed men lay still on the tarmac. The door of the Operations Office stood open, streaming light.

Jimmy Christopher turned quickly to his pilot.

"Get up again at once! Take Miss Elliot to Washington without a stop. Tim, go with her! I'm ordered to stay here and—"

"I'm staying with you, Jimmy!" The dismayed Irish lad leaped down. "Your orders are mine! If you've got to stay, I'm not going!"

Operator 5's lips pinched tight. "Good boy, Tim. I know I can't make you go, but—Diane, you've got to. This plane will get you to Washington soon after dawn. Report to Z-7, Di—report every terrible thing that has happened!"

"I will, Jimmy, but—you're running a frightful risk by staying here!" the girl protested.

"I have orders to follow." Operator 5 stepped back, his eyes shining darkly. To the pilot he commanded: "Take her up!"

He hurried away from the plane even as Lt. Winfield taxied it through a U-turn. With his gun ready, with Tim Donovan at his side, he ran across the field toward the blazing hangars. Momentarily he paused over one of the ground crew, who lay sprawled in the sand—on sand that was red not only with the glare of flames but with the wetness of blood. Three holes pierced the dead man's back.

Grimly Operator 5 sprinted toward the Operations Office. At the open door, he paused again to watch the plane as it rose. Over the cowling, Diane Elliot was looking down, her hair tearing in the wind. She waved an anxious farewell, and Jimmy Christopher answered. As the plane wheeled and began to drive away through the night, he stepped through the door.

INSIDE A small office he stopped short. It was the radio room of the field—and it was a shambles. Panels had been torn from the walls. The delicate, sensitive shortwave equipment had been wrecked by dozens of bullets, fired into coils and condensers. Across the table in front of the wrecked apparatus a man lay, arms outflung—the radio operator. In the center of his forehead shone the round bright hole of a bullet.

Coldly Operator 5 thrust into the office of the Commanding Officer. He heard a moan as he rounded the desk. On the floor, beside files which had been rifled and scattered, lay the trim figure of Major Taynor. Taynor's eyes were staring in terror; his fingers clutched his bloodstained tunic. His breath beat hotly as Jimmy Christopher knelt beside him. His one corded hand clamped hard on that of Operator 5. From his quivering lips burst words of terror.

"The Cheka!… The Cheka!…"

The hand of the wounded officer crushed Operator 5's, then went lax. Jimmy Christopher bent low and pressed his ear to the bullet-riddled chest. He heard no heart-action.

He rose slowly, turned, with a face graven deeply. Striding to the open door he peered across the raided field—at the burning hangars, at the sprawled bodies of the dead, at the tire marks on the sand, tracing the predatory course of the secret killers who had swooped down, committed their terrorism, and fled.

High in the sky the drone of a swift plane came faint and far away—a plane carrying Diane Elliot to safety. And in the midst of a scene of bloody carnage, Operator 5 stood with Tim Donovan at his side, again hearing the dying whisper of a murdered officer of the United States Army:

"The Cheka!… The Cheka!…"

THE VOICE of the President of the United States rang loudly, resonantly, in the closing sentences of the speech he had offered in the vast space of Young Auditorium, in Hartland.

Outside the huge building thousands of cars had choked the streets; sidewalks had massed with men and women mobbing the entrances. Among them the black-uniformed corpsmen of Governor Young mingled; among them members of the secret police shouldered, listening, noting the faces of any who dared speak against their despotic chief. The orders of the Governor, circulated by underground routes, had stipulated that the President must have a crowd—a crowd of thousands—to jeer!

Every gallery was jammed; every aisle filled; every seat of the vast auditorium occupied. Flags festooned the rails and bedecked the platform at the head of the spacious hall. In tiers at the rear of the platform sat scores of men—political advisers, Secret Service men, the retinue of the nation's Chief Executive. Among them, in the forefront, immaculately clad, his eyes alert, sat Operator 5. In a seat at the front of the auditorium sat Tim Donovan.

"…The United States must remain a democracy, must never become the puppet state of a ruler by terror! The dominion which has stifled all liberties in the commonwealth of New Cornwall must not become a blight upon this nation!"

Instantly a thunderous roar of anger exploded in the great hall. Operator 5 saw thousands spring from their seats and shake their fists at the President. Hundreds in the aisles came crowding toward the front while the uproar grew to a deafening intensity.

Secret Service men eased from their chairs behind the President to hurry to his side, but his gesture kept them back. Alone at the front of the platform, cool before the blazing anger of the mob, he peered into the rising tide of wrath.

"Young for President!"

"Young can save us—you can't!"

"You'd let us starve!"

"Young's makin' us rich!"

The angry howls became a chorus of denunciation, and still the President stood calmly facing the turmoil. The thousands in the hall became a roaring, menacing force.

In front of the platform, Tim Donovan sprang to his feet as those around him crushed down chairs to scramble forward. He hurried closer to the President, his widened eyes alert, his heart chilled by the angry growl of the pack.

Suddenly the boy whirled in terror. To the very edge of the platform men had crowded, shouting, shaking their fists, reaching to grasp the legs of the President and pull him down. In the hand of one of them Tim Donovan saw a revolver—a weapon slipped from beneath a coat and turned upward toward the Chief Executive.

Wildly he fought closer, with all his strength struggled to reach the hand that was raising the weapon. The force of the hundreds crushed down upon him. Desperately he twisted, peering beyond the edge of the platform at Operator 5.

Jimmy Christopher jerked to his feet. He had seen Tim Donovan's frantic efforts to reach forward. He saw the boy's wild eyes, saw his lips move. Through the din of the crowd Tim Donovan's warning carried desperately.

"A gun! He's got a gun, Jimmy!"

OPERATOR 5'S hand slipped under his coat as he sprang to the President's side. He peered down into the fighting hundreds at the edge of the platform, and grasped the Chief Executive's arm.

"Get back, sir! For God's sake, back!"

He did not bring his automatic into view but searched the turmoil of movement for a glimpse of the gun Tim Donovan had seen. Suddenly he caught a gleam of metal—a revolver leveled at the President, the hammer pulling back!

He whirled, flinging himself in front of the Chief Executive, directly in line with the gun. And at the instant his body became a shield before the President, the weapon exploded.

The shock of the bullet jarred Operator 5 backward. The report was lost in the ear-numbing howl of the mob. Jimmy Christopher jerked out his automatic as pandemonium broke out on the platform, as Secret Service men sped to surround the Chief Executive. Hot surging pain beat through Operator 5's body from a point near his heart. Two quick bursts of smoke appeared at the edge of the platform.

Twice more the assassin had fired. Twice more, bullets shocked into the body of Operator 5. Straddled, blood spurting from the rips in his coat, his face suddenly white, Jimmy Christopher answered lead with lead.

Once he fired—once, straight at the man with the gun. He

knew, even as he stumbled forward, that his bullet had sped true. Then he dropped to his knees, while bedlam surged around him.

Tim Donovan, his tough hands clinging to the edge of the platform, peered haggardly at Operator 5. He heard Jimmy Christopher's voice, husky with shock and pain: "Take the President away1" He saw Operator 5 sag down—down to the floor. He saw Jimmy Christopher's dripping wounds and a wild cry broke from his lips.

The crushing weight of a thousand men bore upon Tim Donovan as he fought to raise himself to the edge of the platform. In his ears dinned the savage roar of the hostile mob. He was only dimly aware that the President was being hurried from the platform, that Secret Service men were surrounding him with drawn guns. His only thought was for Operator 5. Desperately, with all the strength he could summon, he dragged himself up.

He stumbled to his knees, as a hand caught at his ankle, and peered back at the surf of humans beating around the platform. The howls of enraged men, of terrified women, filled the auditorium—the crashing of chairs, the tramping of countless feet drummed all sound to a higher pitch. Tim Donovan was enveloped by the roar of a storm of wrath as he struggled to the side of Operator 5.

"Jimmy! Jimmy!"

Jimmy Christopher lay unconscious on the platform, his blood staining the boards, the automatic fallen from his hand. His quick action had saved the President from death; but he had stopped the assassin's bullets with his own body.

The shock of the bullet jarred
Operator 5 backward as he
leaped to protect the President!

Tim Donovan grasped his hand, peered around with tear-filled eyes—eyes which pleaded for the help no one would give.

Men were beginning to scramble over the edge of the platform—men with brutal, evil faces. In the crowd Black Troopers were fighting, beating with their guns, clearing their way to the dais. And beneath the festooned flags Operator 5 lay unconscious and bleeding.

TIM DONOVAN struggled to pull him away. The crowd was a mad pack which would trample and kill; human wolves who would crush the life from Jimmy Christopher if he remained in the open. Terrified by the realization, the tough little Irish lad dragged Operator 5 backward across the platform. He thrust chairs aside, cleared the way to the great curtain, then lifted it, disclosing the black space of a spacious stage beyond. Again he closed both hands upon the wrist of Operator 5 and dragged....

Thick darkness enveloped the boy. His cheeks stung with tears as he hooked his hands beneath Jimmy Christopher's arms. He could not carry his friend; his only hope was, somehow, to get Operator 5 to a place of safety. He heard the crashing of breaking chairs in front of the curtain; knew that in a moment the frenzied crowd would come mobbing back. Through the deep gloom, each move desperately quick, he dragged Jimmy Christopher....

Throughout the huge auditorium the storm of terror beat, flooding out the doors, washing into the street. Frantic thousands stormed into the thoroughfares, trampling hundreds underfoot, fleeing from the whirlpool of horror. Snarling motors sang a metallic chorus; cars plowed through the mobs. The assembly had become a barbaric onslaught; merciless, murderous, sweeping away all reason. The guns of the Black Troopers flashed in the light; fists flew; lives became worthless leaves in a storm of blind passion.

And of that frantic turmoil the world knew nothing. At the first outbreak, henchmen of Governor Young in the broadcasting stations had thrown switches.

Through the great curtain of the auditorium, into the heavy gloom, the shriek of the terrorized mob beat. It rang like a threat of doom in the ears of Tim Donovan as he frantically sought cover for Operator 5.

Far at the side of the cavernous space he thrust open a door, found it to be a dressing room. He dragged Jimmy Christopher into the bleak space, slapped the door shut, shot the bolt.

"Jimmy! Jimmy!"

He knelt at his friend's side, with trembling hands sought to find Operator 5's pulse. At first he felt a fast, frantic beat—his own heart. Then he sensed the feeble, erratic pulse of Operator 5—and frantic concern filled him. He sensed that the heart of Operator 5 was failing. He shook Jimmy Christopher's shoulders, and there was no response.

"Jimmy!"

Through the panels of the closed door a gruff voice rang. "Find that kid! Find Operator 5! The Governor wants both of 'em! Find 'em!"

Black Troopers—dark soldiers of terror—searching for their prey!

Tim Donovan brought his small automatic into his hand.

Crouching beside the still figure of Jimmy Christopher, he leveled it at the closed door. His finger trembled on the trigger as he lurked in the dark, guarding his friend. The sounds of the storm of terror beat upon him as his burning hand sought the cold fingers of Operator 5.

"Jimmy! Jimmy!" he sobbed. Again and again: "Jimmy!" Desperate as a trapped animal when no answer came, he huddled beside that still figure, his gun trained unwaveringly on the door....

CHAPTER 6
TERROR BY DECREE

FROM COAST to coast, millions awaited the tabulation of the votes cast in the most bitterly fought Presidential election of the century.

Over a nationwide radio hook-up, political commentators spoke words that flashed over miles of wire, to be reproduced untold times—voices pronouncing the fate of a nation.

"Reports are flooding in from all sections of the country, ladies and gentlemen of the radio audience! Tremendous upsets are in the offing on all Congressional seats. The President, swept into office four years ago by the greatest majority in political history, has suffered powerful losses. It is still too early to predict the outcome, but Governor Young's vote has the volume of a veritable flood!"

In a quiet room of the historic dwelling on Pennsylvania Avenue, Washington, D.C., a grave-faced man sat, while reports streamed to his desk from special telegraph wires, while telephones shrilled in all surrounding rooms, while a radio boomed the latest developments. His shoulders sagged. Dark lines etched his forehead. His eyes shone with an unfamiliar grimness as his closest friend, the chairman of the political party he headed, came slowly to his desk.

"Mr. President, there is still room for hope, but—the outcome is impossible to foretell."

The Chief Executive smiled slowly. "I am not a proud man. The humiliation of a defeat after my first term is one I can shoulder. I will be sorry if my party loses power, but—this nation means more to me than any office, any party. Young's election will mean harm to the United States—fearful harm. That's what concerns me now. That and—"

The President's gaze turned to a gray-clad man standing beside his desk. That man was the Chief of the Intelligence activities of the United States all over the world—Z-7. He had just hurried to the White House. His black eyes were smouldering, and in them lay a deep concern.

"There is still no word, Mr. President," he declared solemnly, "of Operator 5, nor of Tim Donovan. We would be better able to learn what has happened to him if he had fallen into the hands of the Gay-pay-oo in Moscow!"

The President's knuckles rapped the desk. "That young man saved me from death. I should have heeded his advice, yet I could not. As long as Young's power remains unbroken in New Cornwall, our efforts to locate Operator 5, or learn his fate, will face overpowering odds. But—"

An announcer's voice boomed interruptingly from the radio. "Virtually complete returns have been received from the home state of the President. An appalling upset! The state has cast its lot with Governor Young!"

Again and again announcements flashed through the ether, to indicate the tremendous vote piled up by the governor of New Cornwall. "As expected, New Cornwall has voted solidly for Young. Not a hundred votes have been cast against him in the entire state!"

Newspapers, flooding from the nation's presses, carried reports from section after section. "The West is going solidly for Young! Young's lead in the South is piling up! The East is giving Young its endorsement! In all regions the people have overwhelmingly voted for Young! Everywhere it is Young!"

IN HIS sumptuous offices in the State House in Hartland, New Cornwall, Ursus Young sat surrounded by his henchmen. At each announcement from the radio a drunken cheer filled the rooms. As each gain in votes was relayed to the crowds outside the great edifice, the assembled Black Troopers howled their favor, in chorus with the thousands thronging the streets.

In the center of the electrical field of triumph, Ursus Young stood, exuding an evil pride. A raised glass was in his hand.

"There's plenty in the Federal Treasury—plenty more in the pockets of the people—plenty for all of us!"

While midnight blackened the United States, the voices of the political commentators made their crucial announcement.

"Young! Ursus Young of New Cornwall has been overwhelmingly elected to the Presidency!"

INTO A hidden office in the center of Washington, D.C., the news flashed even more quickly than elsewhere. A bulletin stating the result of the national election was placed in the hand of the gray-clad man who sat silent and grim at the back—Z-7. He gave it scarcely a glance. He raised his hands, covered his face. His voice came as a moan through his trembling fingers.

"Now—as never before—we need Operator 5! Where is he? Where is that boy…?"

Word that Ursus Young had been elected President of the United States was flashing into every city and village in the nation. But as for word of Operator 5—there was none.

AROUND THE platform erected on the steps of the Capitol in Washington, on that brisk January day, hundreds of thousands of people mobbed. They formed an unbroken mass, reaching into the radiating avenues, spreading as far as the eye could see. On the rostrum, microphones had been placed to carry, to the far corners of the world, the ceremony about to take place.

The day had dawned when Ursus Young was to assume the office of President, and the hour for the inauguration—high noon—was at hand.

On the platform sat scores of men of the state; foreign dignitaries; officers of the Army and Navy. Nearby the Navy Band was playing, sending martial melody out over the crowd. A chill wind flapped the austere robes of the Chief Justice of the Supreme Court of the United States, seated near the rostrum, whose duty it was to administer the oath of office to the new President. Nearby, his face worn with care, sat the man who would, upon the administration of the oath, cease to hold the highest executive office of the nation.

A President was about to become an ex-President; a citizen was about to become the Chief Executive of a great world power; a new chapter in history was about to be opened. It was an occasion of solemnity.

The dignitaries on the platform stirred as an approaching figure was noted. Ursus Young, President-elect, had left his car, was striding to the platform. He was flanked by four huge men with brutal faces—his bodyguard of deaf-mutes. Secret Service men assigned to him by the Chief of the White House detail followed, relegated to the background. He mounted to the platform, a scowl on his face. Ignoring those who gazed at him, he stepped to the rostrum.

A prolonged cheer broke from the crowd. Young raised an arm in salute and they cheered again. He glanced from the Chief Justice to the President, and his lips curled in contempt.

The President spoke. "Mr. President-elect, it is my duty to turn over to you the destiny of a great government. It is not a government of departments, of legal machinery, nor of documents. It is a government of more than one hundred million human souls whose welfare has been entrusted to you. I pray that God will help you administer your office wisely, your duties justly."

The President offered his hand. Young shook it briefly, his lips still curling with an ugly leer. He turned as the Chief Justice proffered the historic Bible—a Book upon which the hands of great men had rested when assuming the duties of their noble office, a Book hallowed by the touch of past Presidents whose names had carried into tradition and history.

Solemnly, the venerable Chief Justice raised his hand and repeated the Presidential Oath.

"I do solemnly swear that I will faithfully execute the office of the President of the United States and will, to the best of my ability, preserve, protect and defend the Constitution of the United States."

And then Ursus Young committed an act that was unparalleled in the history of the nation. He thrust the historic Bible aside.

Stepping to the microphones, his harsh voice rang into the air surrounding the Capitol, as it rang into every home of the country.

"To the people of this nation, who elected me to this office, I say that I will not raise my hand to the meaningless string of words which have just been babbled upon this platform. I will not preserve nor defend nor protect a scrap of paper which is the cause of the widespread suffering in this country. I declare that I will do all in my power to wipe the Constitution out of existence and establish a new constitution which will give the common people of this country the kind of government and the degree of prosperity they have demanded by electing me!"

STUNNED BEWILDERMENT paled the faces of the ex-President and the Chief Justice. Appalled, outraged, the dignitaries on the platform peered at Young's thick back. He was ignoring them; was speaking to the mob in front. And from that crowd a cheer burst. Over the hub of the nation rose a prolonged, hysterical cry of approbation.

The Chief Justice's blue-veined hand plucked at Young's sleeve. "Sir, under the law, you cannot assume office until you have subscribed to this historic oath."

"Then I will change the law! I will change every musty law on the books, if necessary, to bring a new and vital government to the people of the United States!"

Young bellowed his answer into the microphones which multiplied his words countless times.

"Citizens of this country, the time has come for action. We are done with politics. We are done with bureaucracy. You have demanded a government of power, a government fearless in the face of your problems, and you are going to get it. From this moment on, I will drastically control this country for the good of the common man, for the good of his job and his pocketbook. That is the creed of President Young, and you will see it carried out *now!*"

The ex-President turned from the rostrum, his face white with dismay. The Chief Justice recoiled. Hurriedly they left the platform, while a roar of approval came from the great crowd surrounding the Capitol. In front of the microphones, President Young raised his fists and shouted.

"As President of the United States, I declare this nation in a state of war! Our enemy is poverty! As President I will leave this platform to go straight to my desk in the White House and issue a series of proclamations which will empower me with absolute control of the Federal Government. I intend to wield greater power than any President has ever dreamed of possessing—but I shall wield it for the good of the common man. My speech is ended. I will not use words to fight our battle, but strength! I will not talk—I will act. I'll *make* prosperity—and give it to you. That is my oath of office!"

A cheer that was simply thunderous swelled from the throats of the thronging thousands. Ursus Young, a triumphant leer on his lips, turned from the rostrum.

Immediately his smile faded. He found the chairs behind him empty. Quietly, voicelessly expressing their intolerance of the flaunting of the Constitution, the dignitaries had left the platform. Young stared—and his booming voice broke with fury, with mad egotistical conviction.

"No man is big enough to fight me now! No man will dare raise a word, a finger against me! I—I am the nation!"

INTELLIGENCE HEADQUARTERS WDC-13, the nerve-center of the United States undercover system, was hidden so securely in the center of the Capitol that lifelong residents did not suspect its existence. Closely guarded, it was reachable in only one way. An intricate series of passwords and countersigns was necessary to gain admittance. Only the most trusted of Intelligence agents were equipped to enter the secret inner offices.

Teletype, telephone and telegraph lines linked this Headquarters with hundreds of others scattered throughout the country. Shortwave wireless connected it with secret offices located in all foreign countries. Into it sped thousands of reports from undercover operators twenty-four hours of the day. Eternally vigilant, relentless in its duty, functioning completely unknown to the man in the street, it constituted the most important of all agencies for the protection of the United States.

On the day of the inauguration of Ursus Young as President of the United States, the Washington Chief sat at his desk while reports were brought to him rapidly from the Communications Room. The gray-clad man with the smouldering black eyes read them coldly, in furious amazement. He paused only when a buzzer rasped, and a voice carried out of the inter-office telephone system.

"Ex-Operator Q-6 and a young lady, Miss Diane Elliot, have asked to see you, sir."

"Show them in at once."

Z-7's fingers tapped the desk. The man known as Ex-Operator Q-6, and the girl, were two who enjoyed extraordinary privileges with the Intelligence Service—privileges shared by no one else. In them, Z-7 placed complete trust.

His face darkened with dread at the thought of confronting them. Grimly be continued to read the amazing reports handed him by a shirt-sleeved man who hurried from the Communications Room.

PRESIDENT YOUNG CONTINUES TO ISSUE DRASTIC PROCLAMATIONS—HE HAS ORDERED ALL BANKS CLOSED UNTIL THEIR CONTROL IS ASSUMED BY A FEDERAL BANKING COMMIS-SIONER JUST APPOINTED—PUBLIC INFORMA-TION COMMISSION APPOINTED TO CONTROL

NEWSPAPERS AND BROADCASTING—HAS CALLED A MEETING OF THE GENERAL STAFF AND DRASTIC SHAKEUP IS IMMINENT—NEW PROCLAMATION GIVES HIM COMPLETE POWER TO REGULATE CONDITIONS OF TRANSPORT— ANOTHER DECLARES ALL STATE AND CITY POLICE TO BE UNDER FEDERAL CONTROL OF NATIONAL POLICE COMMISSIONER—DEVELOP- MENTS COMING AT DAZZLING SPEED, GIVING YOUNG VIRTUAL POWERS OF DICTATOR WHICH WILL CERTAINLY BE SECONDED BY LAWS PASSED BY A COMPLETELY DOMINATED CONGRESS.

SWH.

A knock sounded on the door. The girl who entered came to Z-7, extending her hand, and he seized it warmly.

Diane Elliot's radiant beauty was clouded by the grief in her eyes. The pain he saw in them made Z-7 wince: he appreciated it all too deeply. He turned to seize the hand of the quiet-man- nered man designated Ex-Operator Q-6—John Christopher, the father of Operator 5.

"We witnessed the travesty of a Presidential inauguration, Chief," Ex-Operator Q-6 said quietly. "I say frankly that, for the first time, I am glad I am out of the Service. I could not offer any allegiance to that hypocritical political crook, Young."

Z-7'S FISTS clenched hard. "I know Young is playing a game of despicable hypocrisy. On the one hand he gains the support of the people with high promises, which they believe he will fulfill—but his promises are impossible. On the other side he sets up machinery which will make the people the slaves of his dictatorship. If he continues at this rate, the democracy of the United States will cease to exist in a few months! And he *will* continue!

"He has already issued proclamations which give him control of the nation's finances—proclamations which throttle the press and make it an organ of propaganda for him. One by one, he is acting to destroy the fundamental principles of this government. He intends to rule this nation as completely as a Hitler or a Mussolini or a Stalin!"

"You are under his orders, Chief," Ex-Operator Q-6 said quietly. "What are you going to do?"

"That," Z-7 declared coldly, "remains to be seen! I am positive of one thing—he is setting up, even now, a nationwide secret police which will be the most frightful weapon of terror this nation or any other has ever known!"

"Chief." Diane Elliot spoke quietly. "I can't help wondering about Jimmy and Tim. I think of them night and day—and I feel sure they will come back—somehow, someday. Isn't there any news—any news at all about them?"

Z-7's dark eyes glittered. "Absolutely no news, Diane. It's six weeks since I last heard from him—since I spoke to him that night by wireless. The President saw him lying wounded on the platform in Hartland—and that's the last we know. I have done everything possible—I've sent my best men secretly into New Cornwall in search of him. Some of them have never come back—not one of them was able to discover a trace of him or

Tim. The loss of Jimmy Christopher is one of the worst trage-
dies that has ever befallen this country."

Diane asked tensely: "You think—you think he's dead?"

"There's—nothing else to think now."

Diane's face went white. "If Jimmy Christopher is dead," she
declared slowly, "the man who murdered him has just taken over
the chair of the President of the United States. We have a killer
as our Chief Executive. But—I don't believe that, Chief. I don't
believe Jimmy and Tim are dead."

"I hope not, Diane. But—"

"I won't believe it! I won't!"

Z-7 sat silent at his desk. The girl stood with fingers entwined,
her eyes blazing. John Christopher sighed from the depths of
his lungs.

The father of Operator 5 gazed about the secret office with
dulled eyes. Once he had been an active member of the Intelligence Service. A serious wound, suffered in the line of duty,
had forced him into retirement. Two bullets, lying so close to his
heart that no surgeon dared operate to remove them, constantly
threatened him with death. He felt the highest pride in the
achievements of his son. Operator 5 had signally carried on
the work which John Christopher had been forced to abandon.
For six weeks, since the night of the riot in Hartland and the
attempt on the President's life, he had hoped for Operator 5's
return—and had had no word.

"If only Jimmy were here!" he declared grimly. "We'd stand a
chance then of fighting Young somehow. We'd have some hope
of escaping Young's tyranny. If only Jimmy—"

The quiet opening of a door broke into John Christopher's words.

Z-7 gazed at the opened door—and jerked to his feet, pale and rigid. Ex-Operator Q-6 looked through it—and his face flashed white. Diane Elliot peered across the sill—and her hand rose to her parted lips, her glance became transfixed, as if centered on a ghost. With the opening of the door a stunning silence had come into that office.

IN THE frame stood a young man. His face was gaunt, marked with the signs of a severe illness—but it was firm, strong, fearless. The eyes shone with bright determination. He smiled—a slow, warm smile—as he stepped forward. His blue eyes twinkled as he gazed from the Washington Chief, to John Christopher, to Diane.

"Hello, Chief," he said quietly. "Hello, Dad. Hello, Di."

Behind him, a boy appeared. The boy's freckled face was thinned, older after the strain of some ordeal, but his eyes too were shining with spirit. His clothing was tattered and shapeless. His broken-peaked cap was pulled askew over his thickly thatched hair. Yet he grinned—a grin that grew from ear to ear.

"Gee!" he exclaimed. "Gee! Aren't you going to say hello?"

From the lips of Diane Elliot burst a great, glad cry.

"Jimmy! Tim! Jimmy!"

John Christopher, too, blurted the name of Operator 5. Z-7 stood pale, still not daring to believe his eyes, as the girl flung her arms around Jimmy Christopher, sobbing out incoherent words. Then, slowly, a smile formed on the lips of the Washington Chief—and the office became a bedlam of hysterical greetings.

Out of the Communications Room men came running, to grip the hand of Operator 5, to slap Tim Donovan's back. John Christopher hugged his son close, and tears glittered in his eyes. The greetings of the men who crowded around became a booming chorus.

Diane Elliot clung to Operator 5's arm, hugged Tim Donovan until the boy gasped a breathless protest. The tough little Irish lad wrung Z-7's hand, grinning speechlessly. Until the furor subsided, Z-7 remained at his desk; and at last Jimmy Christopher stepped forward with hand extended.

"Operator 5 reporting, sir!"

Z-7 seized Jimmy Christopher's hand. His throat tightened so that he could not speak. He heard Diane exclaim: "I told you he'd come back—I told you he would!" At last Z-7 blurted: "Thank God!" And then: "Operator 5—I want your report at once!"

"Certainly, sir!"

The room grew quiet. Tim Donovan stood proudly at the side of Jimmy Christopher. Diane Elliot curled her hand around that of Operator 5.

He spoke in a husky voice, while undercover agents who had worked with him in the past listened intently.

"Thanks are due to Tim, Chief, that I am able to return—to Tim alone. Until this moment it has been impossible for us to reach you or even get word to you. I've been seriously ill for more than a month—and we started back to Washington as soon as we dared, stopping only long enough to witness the so-called inauguration of President Young before coming to this Headquarters."

Crisply, tersely, Operator 5 told his story. Tim Donovan had stayed at his side in the dressing room of the Young Auditorium until the riot had subsided. Then, the boy had daringly sought his way to the address of K-2, the only Intelligence agent in Hartland who had managed to escape the search of the Black Troopers—the man who had passed the written warning to Operator 5. Together they had brought a doctor to Jimmy Christopher.

For two days Operator 5 had remained in the dressing room, hovering between life and death. Secretly, then, K-2 had transferred him to his own private hiding place.

"Through K-2, while I was still recuperating," Jimmy Christopher continued, "I was able to keep in touch with developments. Diane's report to you, Chief, can be amplified with appalling details. No word has ever appeared in the Hartland press concerning the secret executions. Young's diabolical plague is still killing those who oppose him. The people know nothing of the murders committed by the Black Troopers. For instance, the news of the killing of the physician in the Young Hotel, which I witnessed, was completely suppressed. Not even word of the riot was printed—and the gist of the President's address was hopelessly garbled by Young's corps of censors. I am certain that the attempt to assassinate the President was engineered by one of Young's thugs."

"And that's the situation that will spread over the entire United States!" Z-7 exploded. "No one knows as much about Young's terrorism—no one outside of his own despotic organization—as you do, my boy! We are placed in a fearful predicament. We owe allegiance to the President, and yet the President is a menace to the very existence of the nation we have sworn to defend!"

"Chief—"

FOR THE first time since Operator 5 had begun to speak, there was a movement in the room. A door opened quickly: one of the guards of WDC-13 stepped in. His face was pale, his manner anxious. As every eye turned toward him he exclaimed:

"Chief, he's here! He's coming in now—President Young!"

Z-7's eyes smouldered. He made a sweeping gesture. "Leave this office!" he snapped. "All of you except Operator 5 and Tim Donovan. At once!"

Diane Elliot pressed Jimmy Christopher's hand as she turned to the door, and he smiled at her gravely. Ex-Operator Q-6 was the last to move into adjoining rooms.

As the door closed, Z-7 peered darkly at Jimmy Christopher. In the hallway leading to the inner office heavy steps were sounding.

"Chief," Operator 5 said quietly, "I think we may prepare ourselves for—"

The swift opening of the entrance cut into his words. Into the room strode the huge man who, only a few hours before, had become President of the United States.

He stopped short, peering at Operator 5, and his face became suffused with angry red. Behind him appeared his four brute-like deaf-mutes; and following the bodyguard came two men in uniform. They paused just inside the door.

Young turned to face Z-7, his lips curling. "You are the Chief of the United States Intelligence Service," he declared gruffly, "and you take orders from the President."

Z-7's face went white. "I am the Chief," he answered, shortly.

"Your men are likewise under my orders!"

Z-7 said nothing. Young turned to face Operator 5. He raised a threatening finger as he declared:

"Operator 5, you are summarily dismissed from the Intelligence Service, effective this instant!"

Jimmy Christopher's worn face went pale. Then, slowly, a wry smile began to form on his lips.

"You may order my dismissal, Mr. President," he declared crisply, "but you cannot force me to cease my activities in the name of the Service. Whether I am in the Service or out of it, I will do my utmost to protect and preserve my country."

Young's face colored. "Your orders are to cease from all activities connected in any way with service to the Government—"

"Those orders," Operator 5 declared grimly, "I cannot receive."

Young's huge fist opened and closed. "Operator 5, consider yourself under arrest!"

Jimmy Christopher's face became whiter. "Very well, sir. I am under arrest."

Young indicated his two uniformed henchmen. "This man is Anton Stelzer," he said, pointing one out, "whom I have just appointed Chief Officer of the Law for the District of Columbia. This other man is Samuel Cohu, his assistant. Stelzer! Take Operator 5 into custody at once!"

"Yes, sir!"

The two newly appointed puppets of Young stepped to the sides of Operator 5. He stood unmoving, eyes defiant and fixed firmly on the angry face of President Young.

Z-7, his steps slow and determined, came around the desk to face Young.

"Mr. President, Operator 5 is by far the most valuable undercover agent serving the United States. He has literally saved this country from destruction, not once but several times. He has been honored, as no other man has ever been honored, by the ex-President. I demand to know on what grounds you base his dismissal from the Service."

Young sneered. "I have no need to answer your question. I have orders for you also, Z-7. This Headquarters is to be closed and abandoned within an hour. You are to transmit orders to every other Intelligence Headquarters within the United States, that they also are to be closed. Every man in the Service is to be summarily dismissed. Every branch of this Service is to cease operations forthwith. You, sir, are instantly to issue the orders which will wipe the Intelligence Service out of existence!"

JIMMY CHRISTOPHER'S eyes blazed into those of the President. Z-7 stood motionless, his face white. He was stricken dumb by the words he had heard. The depths of his dark eyes sparkled with the fire of fury and his lips pressed tight

Then he stepped forward and spoke in a firm, level tone.

"Mr. President, I have devoted my life to the organization of the Intelligence Service. It is the chief bulwark of my Government. Hundreds of men under my command have risked their lives without question in the service of their country. They work at small pay, at all hours, in spite of all dangers—in the name of patriotism to the United States. I cannot bring myself to wreck the secret world they and I live and work in. I cannot bring myself to commit such willful damage to the welfare of the United States. I refuse absolutely, Mr. President, to follow your orders!"

Young's heavy fist crashed to the desk. "By God, those orders will be followed out! This Service will cease to exist today whether you relay my orders or not! You, sir, are also under arrest!"

Z-7 stood white-faced at his desk. President Young turned wrathfully to the door through which he had entered. He snapped it open, showed men standing in the corridor—a score of men Z-7 had never seen before. Following the President, they had penetrated to the guarded precincts of WDC-13. Their faces were cold and brutal. They were, Operator 5 realized as he gazed among them, the leaders of Young's dread organization of secret police.

"Clear these offices!" he commanded them. "Drive everybody out of them! Take charge of the communications, the files, every department. You, Captain Critz!"

A square-faced, evil-eyed man stepped forward.

"You are in charge of this Headquarters. You are to transmit orders at once, putting your men in control of every Intelligence unit in the nation. Within an hour the Intelligence Service must cease to exist!"

Immediately the men tramped into the office. They charged at the connecting doors, thrust them open. Turmoil came into the rooms as they began, with drawn guns, to force Intelligence men from their desks. Into the corridor, as Operator 5 and Z-7 watched, the weapons of the secret police forced Diane Elliot and John Christopher. Speedily Young's men tramped through all the rooms, clearing them of every person faithful to the Intelligence Service.

"Guard the doors!" Young thundered. "Admit only men known to you!"

Tim Donovan had been watching Young with blazing eyes. His small hands had curled into fists. His lips trembled with fury. In spite of Operator 5's warning gesture, he stepped forward and snatched at President Young's arm.

"You can't do that to Jimmy and Z-7! They're the finest men in the world! They don't deserve that! You can't—"

Young's massive hand struck Tim Donovan forcibly across the mouth. Stunned, the boy staggered back. Young followed with a second blow which spun Tim across the room and flung him against a bank of filing cabinets. The boy spilled to the floor while the guns in the hands of Stelzer and Cohu covered Jimmy Christopher and Z-7. Tim brought himself up with tears streaming from his eyes, blood flowing from a cut lip.

"Take these men out of here, and the boy with them!" Young ordered thunderously. "Hold them incommunicado! If they resist—you know how to handle them! You have your orders!"

Jimmy Christopher's hand shot out to seize Tim Donovan's. "Steady, old-timer!" He gazed with darkened eyes at Z-7. "I suggest that we go with these men quietly, Chief."

"Very well, my boy."

THE WASHINGTON Chief's answer was scarcely a whisper. He had seen all the rooms cleared of his men; he saw Young's secret police establishing themselves in the Communications Room. Already files were being consulted, teletype machines were clicking—orders were going out to all Intelligence Sub-headquarters ordering a drastic shutdown. In a few swift moments Z-7 had been stripped of his power to control the organization to which he had given the best years of his life.

He shrugged, and stepped beyond the desk. "In spite of all you have done, President Young," he declared levelly, "I still adhere to my oath to preserve the nation and uphold the Constitution you have flaunted."

"Take them away!"

The two officers of the District of Columbia stepped forward. One jerked handcuffs from his pocket, snapped the cold steel rings around the wrists of Operator 5 and Z-7, linking them together. He took weapons from both men.

The other held a leveled gun on Tim Donovan. The three prisoners were shoved toward the door while Young gazed at them leeringly.

They paused grimly on the sill; glanced back, once, at the office now controlled by Young's secret police. Then, guns probing their backs, they strode together along the corridor.

By way of a secret elevator, through secret doors, they were escorted to the street. The carefully hidden approach to WDC-13 was now under the guard of Young's terrorists. They were taken across the sidewalk to a waiting car. Operator 5 and Z-7 were forced into the front seat. Young's chief, thrusting Tim

Donovan into the rear, sat with gun leveled at their backs while his deputy took the wheel.

"The President warned you to come quietly. See that you do!" the chief growled.

Operator 5 sat between Z-7 and the deputy. His lids were lowered, but he was peering about.

The sidewalks were thronged with followers of President Young who had flocked to the Capitol to witness the inauguration. The traffic in the streets was heavy.

The driver of the police car touched a lever, threw a clanging bell into action as they started off. The clamor cleared the way for them through the hundreds of cars. They started off speedily—to imprisonment from which, Operator 5 realized grimly, there could be no appeal.

His nerves tightened as the car whirred along the radiating avenue. He glanced at Z-7 to find the chief's face deathly pale. A glimpse into the rearview mirror showed the gun leveled at their backs, Tim Donovan pinioned to the seat by the outthrust arm of Young's official puppet. The fingers of Operator 5's free hand strayed to his vest pocket....

The car swung away from the brighter light, began to follow a gloomy circling street. Large government buildings were passed—buildings housing Federal Departments which even now were being taken under control by Young's henchmen. On corners here and there newsboys were shouting headline after headline: Jimmy Christopher listened grimly.

SECRET SERVICE REORGANIZED BY YOUNG!

YOUNG TO ENLARGE SUPREME COURT!
YOUNG ESTABLISHES WAR-TIME CENSORSHIP!*

AGAIN THE car swung, into a still gloomier street. Operator 5's elbow pressed a warning to Z-7's side. The prison to which they were being taken was not far now—and it was a destination which would spell their doom. As shadows flicked past, Operator 5 suddenly acted.

His hand shot to the wheel and twisted it. The speeding car careened, as a howl broke from the driver and Chief Stelzer, in the rear seat, was thrown off balance. Deliberately Jimmy Christopher shot the sedan to the curb—directly toward a thick-trunked tree. One swift instant the car plunged, then came a dazing impact. With all the power of its heavy motor, the sedan slammed into the tree.

---

* AUTHOR'S NOTE: The following dispatch was recently distributed by the International News Service:

"Strict government censorship of the American press can be imposed in war time under a bill already prepared by the War Department, Senator Bennett Clark of Missouri told the Senate Munitions Inquiry today.

"Clark placed in the inquiry record a copy of the proposed bill, which will be sent to Congress for enactment at the outbreak of war. Under it, the President can declare paper and printers' ink to be necessary war-time materials and licensed for use. This, he added, would constitute a censorship of the press.

" 'This will give the President absolute control of the press,' said Clark.

"Colonel C.T. Harris, Army ordnance expert, agreed that the bill would empower the President to deprive a newspaper of its material necessities."

The bumper cracked; metal shrieked. The terrific jar spilled the law officer from the rear seat.

"On him, Tim!" rang Jimmy Christopher's desperate command. He glimpsed the boy's wild move in the rearview mirror as he himself whirled upon the driver. He struck twice, swiftly, with his free hand, driving blows which rattled the driver's teeth.

The man at the wheel slid sideward, snatching at his gun. Jimmy Christopher's hand gripped that wrist, and twisted sharply. Bone crunched. The gun spilled down. Another sharp blow shot to the body of the driver, squarely beneath the heart. Operator 5's fingers twisted into the vital nerve-center and the driver stiffened in a paroxysm. As he fell back, Jimmy Christopher twisted to see Tim Donovan fighting desperately in the rear seat, both hands wrapped around the officer's wrist, whipping a gun downward.

"Out, Chief!"

The shock of the collision had thrown Z-7 forcibly forward. His head had met the cracked windshield, and blood was trickling down his face. Dazed, desperate, he slipped out of the car door as Operator 5 followed. Swiftly Jimmy Christopher ducked into the rear seat. His hands closed around the neck of the law officer; quick manipulation caused nerves to snap. With a gasp, Young's henchman went stiff. Jimmy Christopher drew back, pulling the gasping boy after him.

"Keep out of sight!"

He whirled away from the wrecked car, into the darkness of a doorway—the handcuffs keeping Z-7 at his side. Huddled in deep shadow, Operator 5 brought out his pack of master-keys. Quickly he chose one, worked deftly at the mechanism of the cuffs. His third try loosened them.

He tossed the circles of steel away and straightened.

"Stick close! Those men won't stay unconscious long—we've got to move fast! Young will have his secret police looking for us within half an hour! Move, Chief!"

They darted along the deep shadows of the street. With the shrewdness of hunted wild animals, they kept under close cover. Minutes effaced them from the open scene. Under cover of the night, amid the excitement of the city, they vanished....

CHAPTER 7
DIVIDED ALLEGIANCE

THE HUGE, bleak warehouse stood remote from the hub of the humming Capitol. It was a massive brick hulk, situated on an unfrequented street, surrounded by sordid tenements, shrouded by darkness. Inside, the air was black. Each floor was crowded with high piled furniture and boxes. Silence filled it.

Silence, until the grating of a key in a lock rasped through the interior, along the street floor. A heavy door opened slowly, three shadow-figures darted in. Immediately the door closed, and just inside it the three stealthy visitors stood, listening. There was no sound from without, nor any from within until slow steps sounded through the vast darkness.

A bright gleam shot across the stacks of stored household

goods. In the glare the three—Operator 5, Z-7 and Tim Donovan—stared about swiftly. Again they listened; and at last the deposed Chief of the Intelligence Service took a deep relieved breath.

"We're safe. No one saw us come in here. We have lost one Headquarters and gained another."

Operator 5 asked in amazement: "What do you mean, Chief?"

Z-7's lips curved in a grim smile. "My boy, inside this building is a Headquarters more secret than any ever connected with the Service. It has never been used. Years ago I provided it against the most extreme of emergencies—the day when a foreign foe might invade the United States, the danger of fire at WDC-13, any force that might destroy our Central Headquarters. The time has come to use it now!"

"I knew nothing of this, Chief!"

"Nor has any other man in the Service. No one but myself has ever known of it. It is completely covered. No records anywhere show its existence, or indicate that this building is the property of the United States. There's absolutely no clue by which President Young may learn of this place. All these years this secret office has been waiting for this moment. Come with me!"

Z-7 strode along an aisle between the high stacks of crates and household goods. He raised the gate of a freight elevator. Throwing a switch, he sent the great cage crawling upward into darkness. At the seventh level he brought it to a stop, and stepped out. He snapped a switch, and light disclosed another floor crowded to the ceiling with stored goods. He led the way past windows covered with tarpaper through which no gleam of light could penetrate, and paused near a great packing case.

Beside it a grandfather's clock was sitting, dusty, mouldering with age. Z-7 opened its face; swung the hands to twenty minutes past three. A quiet grinding sound followed. In amazement, Operator 5 and Tim Donovan saw the wall of the huge packing case, actuated by a hidden motor, swing outward on concealed hinges; saw that the inside of the door was a plate of steel. Z-7 stepped through and gestured them to follow.

They came to his side, and the metal door slowly ground shut. They stood in darkness until the Washington Chief touched a switch that brought bright light—and an amazing sight.

They stood in a space completely surrounded and concealed by the stacked goods of the seventh floor—a series of small offices constructed of sheet metal. The place was soundless, save for the beat of their heels. Briskly Z-7 led them through room after room, explaining rapidly as they proceeded.

"In this room are duplicates of our most important records. Data on every operator in the Service is on file. This second room contains a complete wardrobe of all the military uniforms of every nation in the world—two of each—as well as various costumes which may be used for disguise. All necessary pigments and makeup materials are also here. In this safe there are secret funds. On the whole, this Headquarters duplicates WDC-13 as closely as possible. The room which I am about to open is the most important of all."

Z-7 UNLOCKED a door, and Operator 5 followed him into a steel-walled compartment remote from the others. In one corner sat an elaborate, sensitive shortwave wireless; in another, a telephone switchboard. Within a special soundproofed booth was a second board on which a score of cams were affixed. Z-7 explained rapidly:

"First, the telephone system here is a special one, supplied by its own power. It can be connected with any telephone in the world—yet it doesn't pass through the Washington exchanges. Special secret wires connect that board with all the principal cities in the country, and through those cities messages may be relayed to any other spot. None of the wires are connected with any of our Sub-headquarters. Governor Young may establish a complete censorship of the nation's telephone system, but he won't be able to trace any calls to or from that switchboard."

"Chief, this is immense!"

"The wireless equipment is of the most sensitive design, able to reach around the world. It too has its own power supply. The replenishing of the storage-battery banks for all these wires is done in another building—which has no apparent connection with this one. Most important of all, my boy, is the microphone system which centers here in this booth."

Z-7 opened the compartment door, took a position in front of the panel. "This is the most valuable of all our devices. I designed it for the greatest possible emergency—an invasion of Washington by enemy forces, and their complete control of our Federal Government. In the event of such an invasion, all our offices would be taken over by the enemy commanders and used as their centers of operation. So, unknown to anyone else in the world—even the President—I succeeded in having microphones installed at strategic points.

"There is, for example, a super-sensitive microphone concealed in the ceiling of my office at WDC-13. Another is in the President's study at the White House. Others are in the Cabinet Room, in the offices of the Chief of the Secret Service and the Chief of the Bureau of Investigation of the Department of Justice. One is installed in the conference chambers of the General Staff in the War Department building. All of them are connected by direct, secret wires, powered by a special supply, to this switchboard and this loudspeaker.

"This, my boy, constitutes a spy system that never sleeps. It is extremely valuable to us now—yet it can be only supplementary to any program of action we map out."

"Gee, Chief!" Tim Donovan exclaimed in wonderment. "You mean you can listen in on anything being said in any of those places?"

"I can." Z-7's hand raised to a cam. "A touch on this contact connects the line between the loudspeaker and the consultation room of the General Staff. A mere movement of my fingers, and—Good Lord!"

He had moved the cam. Immediately a voice sounded inside the soundproofed booth—a heavy, rasping voice which brought a chill to the heart of Operator 5. Snarling words echoed in his ears.

They were listening to the brutal voice of the new President, as he spoke in a room miles away.

"**OFFICERS OF** the General Staff, I have summoned you

here for important orders. I am, I remind you, Commander-in-Chief of the Army and Navy. I have declared the country in a state of war. I intend to take drastic measures to see that my proclamations are carried out. I have learned, gentlemen, that the military mind is loath to accept innovations in method. Therefore, I am giving you my orders.

"To Major-General Douglass, Chief of Staff. Major-General Hurman, Deputy Chief of Staff." Swiftly, President Young continued to read the names and offices of each of the members of the joint board of the Army and Navy, finishing with that of the secretary.

"Receive your orders, gentlemen! You are all, by special dispensation of your Commander-in-Chief, effective at once, demoted from your respective offices to the ranks of Second Lieutenant and Ensign respectively. There, gentlemen, are your written orders!"

A flutter of paper sounded over the line. The voice of an officer burst but in horrified indignation.

"Impossible, sir!"

"Possible—and done!" Young snarled. "I have already appointed a new General Staff, acting upon my powers as Commander-in-Chief, and it will begin functioning at once under my command. In this advice, gentlemen, you will find mentioned the posts to which you are to report for the ordinary duties of your new ranks. I warn you that your comments on these orders may render you liable to heavy punishment for rank insubordination and mutiny! That, I believe, is all!"

Over the wire sounded a heavy step; a door slammed; a

stunned silence followed. Z-7 tipped the cam into neutral and turned to peer, appalled, at Operator 5. Jimmy Christopher's face had gone white.

"Young has taken complete control of the Army and Navy! His new General Staff can be nothing else than a collection of dummies to do his bidding! He'll organize them into a nation-wide patrol to put down all opposition to him!"

Jimmy Christopher stepped from the door, faced the other switchboard. "Chief," he demanded, "is it possible to use these lines to reach all Intelligence men in Washington?"

"It is!"

"Then we must call them—bring them here at once. They will obey you, as their Chief, and come if you order them. It will be a dangerous thing to do, but unless we do it, Young's power will spread until everything we love as part of the United States will be wiped off the face of the earth."

"I'll call them, my boy."

Z-7 stepped to the switchboard. Operator 5 watched him make a connection, heard him speak cautiously. Z-7 gave directions which would bring the man he spoke to—a trusted agent of the Intelligence Service which no longer existed—to this secret rendezvous.

Operator 5 tapped his Chief's shoulder. "There is one man, Chief, not a member of the Service, whom I must see. You can reach him at his home in Washington. He is a physicist connected with the Department of War—Roger Wentling Marlin. Please urge him to keep your orders strictly secret."

"I'll call him."

Jimmy Christopher stepped back to the soundproofed booth. Tim Donovan watched him anxiously as he read the labels above the cam switches of the secret microphone system. Grimly he touched that marked WDC-13. He stood motionless, his dark eyes glowing, as voices issued from the speaker.

"Yes, Captain Critz!"

Operator 5 tensed as he heard the voice of Critz, that cruel-faced chief of Young's secret police—the man whose forces now dominated WDC-13, whose terroristic organization was spreading its tentacles far across the nation at this very moment.

"Special orders for all secret police in Washington! The men known as Operator 5 and Z-7, and the boy known as Tim Donovan, are to be taken prisoners. If any of them resists arrest, he is to be shot. Find them! And instruct all our men that if any of these three is brought in dead—there will be no questions asked!"

WITHIN THE secret steel-walled offices, silence reigned. Hours had passed since Z-7 had completed the nerve-wracking task of telephoning the trusted agents who had been swept from all connection with the Intelligence Service. He had reached them at their homes, by devious connections which could not be traced. He had arranged a secret rendezvous with them all. The moment for the undercover meeting was near.

Z-7 had left the secret offices. At the Chief's desk Operator 5 sat, his eyes darkened with a grim, faraway expression, his mind intent upon a plan. He had made a sheaf of notes, carefully outlined. His face was still wan and drawn from the effects of his illness; his full strength had not yet returned; the nervous strain of his situation was severe.

He glanced at Tim Donovan, on duty inside the cabinet at the microphone switchboard; then rose as Z-7 hastily reentered.

"Most of our men have reported!" the Washington Chief exclaimed. "I have left M-8 on duty at the door. They will all be here in a few moments. You realize, my boy, that this is an almost hopeless undertaking—that we are taking up a fight against a merciless power."

"I realize that, Chief," Operator 5 declared, "and I realize that nothing else is possible."

The door of the soundproofed cabinet opened: Tim Donovan shouldered out breathlessly.

"Jimmy! I've just heard Governor Young give orders to his new Secretaries of War and Navy. He has ordered demoted all Commanding Officers of all posts, camps, airfields, coast-defense units, and naval vessels! In each case he's putting one of his own men in command. I heard him say that he intends to run not only the Army and the Navy, but every police department in the country!"

Z-7 exclaimed: "I'll take that board!" He pushed into the booth.

Operator 5 studied the boy's drawn face intently. Tim exclaimed: "Gee, Jimmy! Young's setting himself up as an absolute monarch of the United States! Fighting him means running an awful chance—but I'm with you all the way!"

"I know it, old-timer. Good boy!" Operator 5 passed his hand wearily across his face. "Before weeks have passed, Tim, the government we've lived under may have fallen. It will mean absolute wreckage of our nation, our homes, our standing among world powers. Young's reign will mean absolutely certain ruin!" Tim Donovan's hand seized Operator 5's anxiously. "Jimmy, you're more worried than you've ever been before. Try to get your mind off of it, Jimmy." The boy grinned beguilingly. "Show me a trick!"

Operator 5 chuckled. "Perhaps you're right, Tim. But our men are coming—I can't take long. The chief and I have got to go out there soon and—" He broke off with a wag of his head. "Okay, boy. I'll show you something that'll keep you guessing—a mental marvel. Listen, I'll give you the total of a series of large numbers even before you decide on what numbers are to be added together!"

"Aw, Jimmy, that's impossible!"

OPERATOR 5'S lips curled in a smile. "I'll demonstrate to you that it isn't. Here's a sheet of paper. Write down a number—any number, in the millions, if you like. Got it down? Now, how many deep shall we make this addition, Tim—shall we add up three numbers like that, or five, or seven, or more? Take your choice."

"Make it five, Jimmy!"

"Okay, Tim." Operator 5 took up a small scratch-pad, wrote upon it so the boy could not see, and tossed it aside. "We'll look at that later. I've written a number on it, which will turn out to be the sum of the numbers you haven't even thought of yet. The one you've already written down is 369,673,454."

"That's right, Jimmy!"

"Now write another one right below it."

The boy placed a second large number under the first, so that the two became:

369,673,454
181,963,482

"Now, Tim," Jimmy Christopher smiled, "I'll write one down, because I've got to make the answer come out right. We'll alternate on the rest until we have five rows. Here we go."

Rapidly, as though writing numbers at random, Operator 5 placed his figures under those written by Tim: 818,036,517.

"Your turn, Tim."

The boy wrote, with his tongue squirming in the corner of his mouth, another number: 675,934,432.

"Now this time I've got to write a number, Tim, which will make my answer right—the answer I've already written on the other sheet. That, you must admit, is quite a task in mental arithmetic. But I don't have to think hard about it. I can do it without a second's hesitation. Here it is." Rapidly Operator 5 wrote the fifth and final line of the addition: 324,065,567.

"Now, add 'em up, Tim!"

The boy worked eagerly at the sum, striving to make no mistake. When he raised his eyes, the job complete, Operator 5 reached for the second slip of paper. They boy stared in amazement at the number Jimmy Christopher had written on it at the very beginning of the trick. It was: 2,369,673,452.

"Jimmy—gee! That is the right answer! It checks with mine!" the boy blurted. "You wrote it down right after I put down just the first line, too! How'd you do it, Jimmy? You really couldn't add it all up in your head so fast as we went along and make it come out right that way!"

"No, Tim—it's only a trick, really. You can do it yourself. Listen, you wrote the first number, then I foretold the answer on another slip! Right? I did that according to a system I'll explain in a minute. Then you wrote the second number, I wrote the third, you the fourth, and I the fifth. Now then—each time, under every number you wrote, I put one which added up to nine. See here."

Operator 5 pointed it out to the amazed boy. "Your second number begins 181. Under the one I wrote eight. Eight and one are nine. Under the eight I wrote one. Under the one, eight again. Each number I wrote, added to the one directly above it, made a total of nine. Check the third line, Tim, and you'll see that's true."

"That's right, Jimmy!"

"Then you wrote another long number. Again I made nines by addition. Under your six I wrote three. Under your seven I write two. Under your five I wrote four, and so on. That's half the trick. The other half is knowing how the answer must come out. That's simple, too.

"In this case, I simply subtracted two from the first big number you wrote. I put the figure two in front of that big number as the answer, followed it with the rest of your first number, finishing with the original, *less* two. Get it?"

"Not quite, Jimmy!"

"Then follow this. Your original number was 369,673,454.

The last number in the row is four. From that four I subtracted two, making it two. I placed the two in front of your original number, making the answer 2,369,673,452. Got it now?"

"Sure! Say, that's easy! But why did you subtract two, Jimmy? It works out that way, I know, but—"

"The number you subtract, then place in front of the original, depends upon the number of lines of figures in the entire addition. You must determine before you begin how many deep the sum will be. If the addition is three deep, you subtract one, according to this system, to make it come out right. If it is five deep, as ours was, you subtract two. If it is seven deep, subtract three—if nine, subtract four. You can make the addition as long as you please if the length is decided upon before you start!"

"Gosh!" the boy exclaimed. "I didn't see how you could possibly do it, Jimmy—but it's easy when you know how."

"Exactly, Tim. So are most things. Try it a few times, and—"

"My boy." Z-7 had hurried from the microphone switchboard to the entrance of the secret offices; now he strode to the desk. "The man you asked me to send for—Mr. Marlin—is here. We have kept him apart from our secret agents. You can see him now, if you wish."

Operator 5 came to his feet quickly. "Please show him in!"

A BROAD-SHOULDERED man with shaggy gray hair entered the office slowly and uncertainly. Operator 5 drew a chair for his bewildered visitor—noting as he did so that Z-7 and Tim had retired to an adjoining room—and Marlin took it while searching his face. The gray-haired man asked cautiously:

"Why have I been brought here—with such secrecy?"

Operator 5 answered briskly: "You are a scientist, and you have spent your life in the service of the Government, Mr. Marlin. Administrations have come and gone, but have meant little to you—you have continued your work uninterrupted. We of the Intelligence have been kept informed of it. It is true, is it not, that you have recently perfected a radical type of broadcasting equipment which radiates radio waves of a new type?"

Marlin looked astounded. "I had supposed that my results were secret! I had no idea!"

"The War Department informs us of such matters. I do not know the details. Your diagrams and charts are under secure lock and key in the War Department building. You have access to them?"

"No!" Marlin exclaimed. "I—I have been discharged by President Young. Why, I do not know. The new Secretary of War informed me that younger men were needed. Yet I cannot believe my services can mean so little."

Operator 5's eyes clouded. "You were discharged to make room for one of Young's hirelings, Mr. Marlin! You cannot reach your charts now. But you can reproduce them. They are thoroughly familiar, down to every detail, in your memory, I suppose? You will be able, if provided with the proper parts, to erect a broadcasting station which will send out the new eddy currents instead of straight waves?"

"Yes, but—"

"A station of that type, once erected, will be able to cover the entire United States, if powerful enough, isn't that correct? It can be tuned in on any radio of any present design. But—and this is the point—no direction-finders will be able to locate it! If it is securely hidden, it can broadcast without fear of its location being detected."

"That's true. But why do you want one of these stations erected?"

"As the very best means we know of telling the people of the United States the truth about the tyrant Young!"

Marlin came to his feet in dismay. "To be used against President Young? No! I cannot lend myself to any plot against the United States Government, no matter who heads it!"

Jimmy Christopher's face grew grave. "Mr. Marlin," he asked slowly, "do you know the whereabouts of your son Grant?"

Pain came into the old man's eyes. "No—no, I do not. Six weeks ago he wrote me from Hartland, New Cornwall. He was born there; was politically ambitious. He was determined to fight Young at the polls. I have had no word from him since the election. I have been dreadfully worried, but I'm sure—"

"He is your only son?" Operator 5 inquired quietly.

"Yes."

Jimmy Christopher's tone became lower. "Mr. Marlin, I have tragic news for you—news I wish I could spare you. I know that Grant was very dear to you, that you have been devoted to him. I'm afraid that you will never hear from him again.

He is—"

"Dead?" Marlin choked out the word. "Grant is dead? How do you know?"

"He is dead. He was shot. He was executed by order of Governor Young. He lies now in an unmarked grave, in a lonesome spot in the woods, outside Hartland, with four others who were shot down at the same time. One of them, I believe, was the girl he loved."

AS THE stricken old man stared, Operator 5 drew a wallet from his pocket. He extended it to Marlin. The scientist's fingers trembled as he withdrew the identification card it contained. Softly Jimmy Christopher continued:

"I saw him shot down. I saw Young's firing squad plunder his body of that wallet, empty it of money and throw it aside. I found it on the spot where he lies buried. The despot Young is as guilty of the death of your son as if he pulled the trigger with his own finger. I am telling you the strict truth, Mr. Marlin. And that's why I'm asking you to aid me in a fight to remove that murderous tyrant from the President's chair."

Marlin stared into the face of Operator 5. He fondled the wallet, mumbled, "I—I can't think! I can't believe—such a horrible thing. Yet—" He broke off and his kindly blue eyes flooded with tears. Operator 5 rose quietly and stepped from the room, leaving the old man alone.

Immediately a step sounded behind him—Z-7's. The Washington Chief seized Jimmy Christopher's arm, his eyes glowing darkly.

"They are all here, my boy—the men of the Service. They are waiting for us."

Grimly Jimmy Christopher said: "Lead the way, Chief. There's no time to lose!"

Z-7 strode briskly to the hidden entrance of the suite of steel-walled offices. They stepped together into the gloom outside the secret door, followed the wall deeper into the vast room. Far beyond the elevator a space was cleared. A packing-box was placed near one side, forming a crude platform. In front of it men were standing—scores of men, silent, waiting, their faces glinting darkly.

Briskly Z-7 and Jimmy Christopher strode to the makeshift platform. The cleared space was silent until Z-7's edged voice carried through the gloom.

"You men," he began quietly, "know that the United States Intelligence Service no longer exists—as a department of the Federal Government. You have served me, your Chief, fearlessly and capably in the past. You have had only one creed—to protect and preserve your nation. I have called you here to ask your continued allegiance—to stand at my side in a secret fight against the man who threatens to wipe the United States out of existence."

All eyes stared at Z-7. He continued ringingly, his eyes blazing with a light of defiance.

"Before I go further, I warn you that this is organized treason. This, gentlemen, is the fomenting of a revolution. We will move in constant danger of arrest by President Young's new secret police, in danger of imprisonment without trial, in danger of execution without the slightest hope of appeal. All of you, if you follow me upon our determined course, will face the penalty of spies at work in an enemy country in time of war. We will be facing peril at every turn while fighting *for* our country and *against* a terroristic dictator. We will face death.

"If any of you men wish to withdraw, if any of you wish *not* to fight this secret war at the side of Operator 5 and myself—this is the moment when you must speak!"

No word came from the lips of the listening soldiers of secrecy.

"You who stand here signify, by your remaining, that you pledge yourselves to fight the despot. You declare your loyalty anew to our crumbling nation, though it cost you your lives!"

Not a man moved.

CHAPTER 8
THE HOODED FOE

Z-7 GAZED grimly into the faces of the men confronting him. There was silence in the vast room. Each man realized that, beyond these walls, the terroristic power of Young was spreading hourly, that it was a force which would wipe them all out of existence if their operations were discovered. Secrecy alone shielded them from the threat of that power. And signifying their allegiance to their Chief by their very silence, they waited for him to resume.

"The United States Intelligence Service no longer exists. But we have created, at this moment, a new undercover agency which must grow in the soil of secrecy, in the shadow of danger. We are, gentlemen, the Minutemen of our Government, as truly as the patriots who built the United States on the battlegrounds

129

of the American Revolution. Bound by that loyalty, let us fight as long as we live!"

Z-7 turned from the platform. Operator 5 took his place before the silent secret agents. His eyes shone brightly as he faced them.

"Comrades, you have in the past worked at my side to preserve our nation from destructive forces. We have united in fighting powerful espionage combines, in repulsing armed attacks, in stifling revolution. Now we find ourselves in the very position of those we have, in the past, fought. We have battled revolutionists, and now we are ourselves revolutionists. We have stamped out plotters against the Government, and now we are ourselves plotting against the Government—of the tyrant Young."

With impressive silence the men listened.

"If President Young is the nation, we are enemies of our own country! It is not only that we have pledged defiance to his dictatorship. We are unalterably opposed also to all the dangerous, subversive forces that are allied with him. Behind him, now, stand rings of destructionists whose only aim has been to destroy the United States. Over all the country, un-American organizations are hailing Young as their new leader—hailing him as their unholy messiah who will make the United States a nation of the past—a nation which, once crushed down, can never rise again!"

Jimmy Christopher's voice rang clearly; his eyes blazed with fervor.

"These subversive forces have been at work against our nation for years. We have until now succeeded in restraining their destructive activities. Under the regime of Young, they are seizing the opportunity to tear down this great nation built of the blood and sinew and courage of our forefathers!" *

The undercover agents were listening to Operator 5's every word intently.

"A double danger faces the people of the nation!" he continued ringingly. "On the one hand there is the despotism of Young backed by the destructionist organizations. On the other hand there is no organized opposition to Young. That very lack of organization is why we are here tonight, in secret meeting.

---

* AUTHOR'S NOTE: As an example of the dangerous radical activities going on in the United States, the following excerpts from news dispatches published late last year are significant.

"Major General Smedley D. Butler today spent more than three hours 'before the Congressional Committee on Un-American Activities at the Bar Association, 42 West 44th St., New York City.

"According to reports that leaked through closed doors of the unexpected session, the former officer of Marines told how he had rejected the role of Fascist dictator of the United States in a $3,000,000 plot to overthrow the Government.

"Gerald C. MacGuire, Wall Street bond salesman and principal target of General Butler's charges, denied vehemently that he had waited on General Butler as agent of a group of wealthy New York brokers making a proposal that he organize an army of 500,000 veterans to march on Washington and overthrow the Government.

"Representative Samuel Dickstein of New York, vice-chairman of the Committee, said: 'From present indications General Butler has the evidence correctly. There is much more to this than has been disclosed.'"

We must organize against Young, or the nation is doomed. Disunited, those who oppose Young are powerless before him. Working together under the command of Z-7 means our only hope of rescue!" *

GRIMLY JIMMY CHRISTOPHER declared: "I have drawn up a plan of action that will carry our purpose to all those in the nation who dare fight Young. Secretly, we must spread our strength to the four corners of the United States. We most work swiftly, desperately, to knit together our secret sentinels in an

---

* AUTHOR'S NOTE: The following statement was made recently by an investigator of radical organizations within the United States, whose identity cannot be revealed here. He says, of these un-American movements:

"Their political appeal to discontent, if and when conditions become ripe for Fascist enterprise, cannot be overlooked. As symptoms of the kind of organizations which afflict almost all the major industrial countries in the economic crisis, they are ominous.

"The Nazis, we venture to observe, came to power in Germany, not because they were tolerated by the Government but because their enemies were too disunited to defeat them. Mussolini's Black Shirts achieved power because a weak Government refused to prevent their lawless violence in first destroying the labor and peasant organizations. Already in the United States, as in other countries, the Government shows the same ominous attitude toward incipient Fascism.

"Countless variegated groups move on toward Fascism. The number of their adherents grows. They are disunited, uncertain, with dozens of vague aims, and no one wants to pull their common interests together. But so was Germany split into dozens of wandering parties—before Hitler."

undercover army. We must prepare, beginning at this moment, for the signal which will turn us united against the dictatorship which is stifling our freedoms and our traditions!

"Orders, gentlemen!"

In an incisive voice, Jimmy Christopher read the designations of half a score of the undercover operators present. "You constitute the Sentinels of the Army!" Following another list he declared: "You are the Sentinels of the Navy!" A third list and: "You are the Sentinels of Morale, charged with the building up of our spiritual power through secret broadcasts, secret issues of newspapers—in a word, propaganda against Young!

"I have special written orders for all of you, which will take you into every state, every principal city of the country, on this secret work. These tasks are highly dangerous. Most perilous of all is a special mission which will, I hope, establish a personal spy-system at the very heart of Young's secret organization of police. For the man who undertakes it, it means inevitable imprisonment, perhaps death. It is, I warn you, gentlemen, virtual suicide. I ask for a volunteer!"

Immediately a score of men stepped forward, raised their hands. With grim admiration, Jimmy Christopher gazed into their determined faces. He pointed at a clean-cut young man, with fearless eyes, who had responded an instant ahead of the others.

"T-3, I accept you as volunteer for the special secret mission. Sentinels! You will remain to receive your written orders from Z-7. You will begin operations at once. In the name of our great nation, gentlemen—good luck!"

Jimmy Christopher stepped from the platform as the men crowded forward around Z-7. At his signal, T-3 followed him. Out of sight of the others they paused. Operator 5 declared crisply:

"I warn you again, the task for which you have volunteered may cost you your life. It is highly necessary for us to establish a spy inside Young's secret police. I intend to attempt it myself—but I need help. My plan is one which will, if it succeeds, place me at the very nerve center of the secret police. It will put me in a position of great advantage to our cause—but it may mean your death."

T-3 smiled slowly. "I'm more than willing. You'll be facing far greater danger yourself. I'm ready to follow your orders now."

Operator 5 seized the secret agent's hand. "I knew you'd do it. Let's not waste a moment."

Reaching the old grandfather's clock, he opened the face, adjusted the hands to the contact position, and the steel-lined door swung open. T-3 followed him briskly into the inner office. There, beside the desk, the wallet still in his blue-veined hands, the scientist Marlin was standing.

The old man's eyes were shining with cold fury; his clenched fists were trembling with determination. Operator 5 approached him slowly, and suddenly Marlin spoke.

"I have made my decision! I'll aid you to the limit of my ability! And I'll stop at nothing—nothing to crush Young's power. I am under your orders!"

THE MAN with the scarred face sat hunched at a greasy-topped table in a cheap restaurant not far from the Capitol in Washington. He was unkempt, unshaven; his eyes were red-rimmed and bleary. He was one of hundreds who visited this restaurant, seemingly unaware that it was the secret approach to the hidden offices which once had been WDC-13 but were now the Headquarters of the dread secret police.

The scarred individual, as he ate, talked to the young man who had entered with him—a man in sailor's uniform, with ruddy face and flaxen hair.

"Young? He's nothin' but a political crook!" His voice was so loud that all eyes in that steamy room turned to him. "He's goin' to fill his pockets out of the Federal Treasury with plenty. He's robbin' the people, that's what he's doin'."

The sailor answered: "He broke the skipper. The new Commander is one of Young's dummies. I think you're right."

The man with the scarred face glanced around defiantly. At a table against the wall he noted one who peered at him searchingly. The latter was dark-faced, with eyes as black as a rat's. He continued to eat while the scarred man and the sailor paid their checks and went out. Then he rose from his place instantly and followed.

The pair who had dared voice their denunciation of the President stepped into a taxi. It carried them quickly away from the center of the city. The scarred man glanced back, noted that another cab was following. Nothing was said until they reached a gloomy, remote section, when a word from him stopped the car. They alighted, paid their fare, and walked together along the bleak street.

Apparently they failed to notice that the second taxi had also

135

Operator 5 leaped upon
T3—striking with his gun!

stopped; that the small man with the snaky eyes, who had overheard their conversation in the restaurant, had alighted. They
turned a corner—and instantly stepped into the shelter of the
first doorway.

Quick footfalls told them their shadower was approaching.

They were deep in gloom when the evil-eyed man appeared. Swiftly they sprang upon him.

Quick, deft blows of the scarred man struck him down. Rapidly, then, they lifted the unconscious burden, knocked peculiarly on the door which had sheltered them. It opened at once.

They entered a vast, dark space filled with stored household goods, and carried their man to the elevator. At the seventh floor they lifted him out, dragged him to a large packing case, beside an old grandfather clock. They adjusted the hands of the clock, entered the hidden offices, and closed the way behind them.

Tim Donovan, his eyes wide with concern, followed as they went into the wardrobe room, where they placed the unconscious man in a chair. Immediately they turned to two sinks, and with special soap cleaned the makeup from their skins. The scar of the one washed off. When they turned back, their faces completely transformed, they smiled with grim satisfaction.

They were Operator 5 and T-3.

"Gee, Jimmy!" the boy exclaimed. "What're you going to do?"

"This man," Operator 5 answered, gesturing to his captive, "is one of Young's secret police. We baited him, Tim—tricked him into shadowing us. I intend to become that man."

Quickly Jimmy Christopher searched the secret agent's clothing. He found a card in the victim's pocket. On one side it bore a black capital letter Y—nothing else. On the other it bore a number 564, and written initials. Finding nothing else of importance, he placed it aside, and turned to the door as it opened.

Z-7 STRODE in, white-faced. "My boy, the Sentinel at the

door told me you were here. H-4 has just telephoned a startling report. President Young, by special proclamation, has enlarged the Supreme Court of the United States from nine members to twenty-one. His twelve new appointees are his political dummies. They outnumber the original nine, they'll be able to override any decision of the true Justices. This means that any despotic law Young may choose to force through Congress will be upheld by the Supreme Court!"

Operator 5 declared gently: "I expected that, Chief. Now, at this moment, the law of the United States is Young's will—nothing else!"

Z-7 declared: "There is another report, from D-9. In some quarters there are whispers of an attempt to impeach Young. D-9 has determined that such a move will be impossible to carry out. Congress will be afraid to attempt it—not only because it will be political suicide, but because they fear the secret police, who are everywhere, even in the Congressional halls. It's a certainty that if any member of Congress breathes an intention of proposing to impeach Young, he will mysteriously disappear—either that or contract the plague!" *

---

* AUTHOR'S NOTE: The Constitution prescribes that the House of Representatives shall have the sole power of impeachment and that the Senate shall have the sole power to try all impeachments. In ordinary cases the President or President *pro tempore* of the Senate presides, but when the President of the United States is on trial, the presiding officer must be the Chief Justice of the United States Supreme Court. A two-thirds vote is necessary for conviction. The President, Vice-President or any civil officer of the United

"Our men," Operator 5 inquired crisply, "have reported their movements?"

"Yes. They have reached certain Army posts and Navy yards—I have the detailed information. They are secretly getting in touch with all whom they know to be enemies of Young. Slowly our organization is building. But it will be a long and dangerous job, my boy. Sometimes I'm afraid we can never hope to succeed."

"We've *got* to succeed, Chief! If we don't—!"

Jimmy Christopher broke off ominously, his eyes darkening. With sudden determination, he turned to a table behind which hung a mirror. He placed before him makeup materials—special pigments, invisible glue, hair dye, bits of fish skin—the substances from which he was determined to create a new man in living masquerade.

Z-7 returned to the inner office, but Tim Donovan and T-3 watched in amazement. Operator 5 stripped to the waist—disclosing the welted scars of the bullets which had felled and almost killed him in Hartland. He studied the face of his unconscious captive carefully. Then swift, deft work brought about a

States may be impeached for "treason, bribery or other high crimes and misdemeanors." Since the organization of the Federal Government there have been only eleven impeachment trials before the United States Senate, and of these only three resulted in conviction. The two most famous cases are those of Justice Samuel Chase of the United States Supreme Court in 1805, and of President Andrew Johnson in 1868.

magic result. Before the eyes of the two who watched, he transformed himself into a different man.

His skin became darker. His hair became black, his eyebrows heavier, and shaggy. He produced lines around his eyes; changed the contour of his mouth. With the utmost care he duplicated, bit by bit, the features of Young's secret policeman. Last of all, he made sure that the scar on the back of his right hand was completely covered with opaque pigment.

With T-3's help, then, he carried his unconscious captive into an adjoining room, removed the man's clothing. Tim Donovan, watching the connecting door, saw the same man, apparently, reappear—in full possession of his faculties.

"Will I pass, Tim?" the voice of Operator 5 asked.

"Gee, Jimmy—you look exactly like him! You're not like yourself at all! I'd never think it was you if I hadn't seen you do it!"

Operator 5 smiled slowly and faced T-3. "One more step in the plan," he declared gently. "The next may mean death for you, T-3. Are you still willing to play the gamble with me?"

"I'm with you to the end, Operator 5," T-3 answered firmly. "To the end!"

AT THE door of the historic White House, on Pennsylvania Avenue, a heavy sedan stood waiting. It was the special car of President Young: constructed of armor plate no bullet could penetrate; shatterproof glass. Inside, in special pockets, were firearms. It was literally a rolling fortress Young had provided for his protection.

Out of the entrance strode President Young, accompanied as always by his bodyguard of deaf-mutes. He entered the car with two of them; the other pair shifted to another car. Both started toward the gate—which was guarded by more of Young's private henchmen. The President was on his way to the Treasury Building, there to confer with his puppet who acted as the Secretary. With him Young carried a new proclamation by which he intended to secure vast sums from the Treasury, for the purpose of financing his gigantic system of patronage dummies.

The Presidential car passed through the opened gate, into the street. On the opposite side of the thoroughfare a light coupé was sitting. As the heavy sedan turned, the door of the coupé opened and a young man sprang into the open. He held one hand under his coat—a hand gripping a gun—as he sprinted toward Young's car. He was T-3—taking the first step of the dangerous mission planned by Operator 5.

On the near curb, a second man—dark-featured, hard-eyed—watched T-3 spring toward the Presidential sedan. Quickly his hand jerked to his arm-pitted automatic. He flashed the weapon up and shouted, "Stop him! He's trying to kill the President!" He fired three times swiftly—aiming deliberately over T-3's head.

Before the deaf-mutes in the sedan could realize what was happening, Jimmy Christopher, masked by his disguise, leaped into the street. T-3, in mock terror, whirled to confront him. Operator 5 leaped upon him, striking with his gun. Young, startled, peering through the bulletproof glass, saw the dark man lashing desperately with the weapon. So cleverly did Jimmy Christopher manipulate that his blows, though harmless, seemed to carry murderous force.

T-3 cried out and dropped into the street. Instantly Operator 5 was upon him. At the same moment the door of the sedan burst open and Young's burly bodyguards leaped out. They seized Operator 5's shoulders, dragged him back, gripped their guns by the butts and swung savagely at T-3. No pretense in the force of *their* blows. They struck T-3 mercilessly; and when they rose, the Intelligence man lay bloody and unconscious.

Jimmy Christopher repressed his cold fury; forced himself to carry through his part. "He tried to kill the President! I saw him! Thank God I stopped him in time!"

Out of the car stepped President Young, a scowl darkening his brutal face. "Take him away!" he commanded gruffly. "Throw him in jail! I'll take care of him later!" His bodyguards dragged T-3 into the second of the two cars, and the doors clacked shut upon him. Young growled, beneath his breath, dread words, which Jimmy Christopher caught.

"A firing squad will finish him!"

GRIMLY OPERATOR 5 stepped close, while the guns of two bodyguards covered him. A crowd was beginning to gather in the street. President Young glared at Jimmy Christopher. But his eyes brightened with grim satisfaction at sight of the card Jimmy Christopher drew from his wallet.

"You see, I am of the secret police, Mr. President," Operator 5 declared in a whisper. "I've been watching this man. He's one of the discharged Intelligence agents. I am happy that I was able to keep him from killing you!"

Young blinked. "Get into the car!" he commanded. Promptly Operator 5 obeyed. Young followed him in. The heavy sedan turned back toward the gate of the White House, passed the guards, swung to the entrance. At the President's command, the disguised Operator 5 entered the historic building.

He walked along the corridor hung with oil portraits of past Presidents—statesmen who had labored to build a great nation, a nation the dictator Young was destroying with drastic decrees. He entered the historic study to which, on previous occasions, he had been gratefully summoned to receive honor for services rendered his country—a study occupied now by a man more destructive than any force which had ever threatened the national safety.

Young stepped behind the desk, still holding the identification card Jimmy Christopher had given him; Operator 5 stood at attention.

The President drew a telephone close; called a number. "Shapi!" he snapped. "You're in control of all broadcasting and all newspaper publication. There has just been an attempt to assassinate me. News of it has got to go out all over the country at once. The story is to say that the assassin was hired by a capitalistic organization which we are going to break up. You are to say that I struck the man down and took the gun away from him with my own hands. This is a chance to strike at the big-money men and to make a martyr—you know how to handle it. Get it out at once!"

Young pushed the telephone away, peered once more at the identification card. Taking from his desk a locked metal dossier-box, he consulted its entries. His stubby finger—a finger which had pointed death repeatedly at his opponents—paused on a line—and he glared at Jimmy Christopher.

"You are Donn Doman, Sergeant of the Secret Police. You have done excellent work. It is my pleasure, Sergeant Doman, to promote you to a Lieutenancy, effective at once. You are to take on your duties as assistant to Captain Critz immediately. You will work out of the former Intelligence Headquarters. Lieutenant Doman, I want you to know and tell all your comrades that Young treats his men right!"

FURY CHILLED Operator 5's heart, but he forced a smile. "Thank you, Mr. President!" he exclaimed. "This will be an inspiration to the whole secret police! We are with you to a man!"

"You," Young said, blunt finger leveled, "are to work on a special case, Lieutenant Doman. I have had reports that all the ex-Intelligence men are organizing against me. I want to know where they meet, what their plans are. I want them stamped out, you understand—and every damned one of them brought to me! By God, I'll finish them all off with a firing squad!"

Tight-lipped, Operator 5 answered, "Yes, sir!"

"Damned strange things have been happening," Young went on, "and I intend to find out what they mean. All over the east, the secret police have been reporting storage batteries stolen out of cars. Hundreds of them! Why? I want to know! Four broadcasting stations have been raided and almost dismantled—certain parts carried off. Why? Arms and ammunition have disappeared out of armories all over the country. Why? Trouble is being stirred up by mysterious organizations which show themselves only at night. I want the leaders of those organizations!"

Jimmy Christopher repressed a tight smile. He might have

answered, "These are the operations of the Secret Sentinels, Mr. President, who have sworn to drag you off your dictator's throne."—But he did not.

"I have reports," Young continued with a snarl, "about these strange bands of men from all over the country. They wear black robes and black hoods. They're everywhere. They take orders from some hidden Headquarters. They're spreading sedition against me—attacking my government. And they're growing in numbers every day. You are to work with Captain Critz to stamp this dangerous element out—to kill them off—all, all of them! The people of this country must not know a single word of what happens—but the Black Hoods must be exterminated!"

Operator 5, his throat constricting, answered: "Yes, sir!"

"That's all!"

He turned to the door. Thinking of T-3, lying beaten in the street—T-3, whose bravery had helped him reach the center of the secret police system of Young—his blood pounded with determination. He pictured Z-7, at the secret Headquarters, listening over the microphone system to the words just uttered in this study—and pressed back a grim smile of satisfaction.

As Lieutenant Doman of the secret police, he had been ordered to stamp out the Black Hoods; as Operator 5, he was the leader of those hooded Secret Sentinels!

CHAPTER 9
SENTINEL JUSTICE

BRIGHT STREET lights glowed up and down the clean, broad thoroughfares of the village of Faber. The center of the city was a beautiful little park. Surrounding it lay hundreds of neat, picturesque homes; and dominating the scene in the background rose the white stone buildings of the Faber Corporation. In all the country, this village was without parallel—blessed with the benefactions of the great industrialist and philanthropist, Edward Faber, who had gathered a contented community of workers around him.

He had built great cotton mills and deeded them to the men and women who worked at the machines. He had set up an impartial organization whereby each worker shared alike in the profits of the prosperous plants. He had built and sold homes at cost; had provided stores which sold without profit. He had, in short, built a community of and for its members; in which politics played no part—and he had died leaving his memory beloved.

Faber stood marked as the only community in the country which had, in the Presidential election, voted *en bloc*, without a single dissenting voice, *against* the candidate Young! And now a blight poisoned the air of Faber—at its entrances red signs reading: Village Quarantined! warned travelers away. Homes were hushed with the anxiety of a dread illness: scores of the modest little houses bore the crimson mark of the pestilence. Men and

BLOOD REIGN OF THE DICTATOR

Terror broke out in the ranks of the black-uniformed troops; they were surrounded by grim, robed men!

women were wasting away in the grip of the horrible plague which had spread from the borders of New Cornwall, hard by.

Tonight, as the clock in the white church steeple tolled midnight, the tramp of marching feet sounded in the quiet village. Out of the darkness, troops advanced—a squad of hard-faced men wearing the black uniform of the Special Health Corps.

As the ominous rhythm disturbed the serenity of the night, doors opened, windows raised, men and women came into the street with fear striking at their hearts. To the very center of the village green the commander led his Black Troops. And toward the dark formations, the townspeople came hurrying fearfully.

To their worried questions, the Commander made no reply. He merely waited while huge U.S. Army trucks, which had followed the squad, rumbled along the edge of the green and stopped at the front of the cooperative stores.

From the trucks more Black Troops descended. They charged at the doors; used the butts of their rifles as battering rams. The managers of the stores, rushing to protest against the vandalism, were thrust back by the rifles of other troopers. The doors crashed down; and into the stores the dread troopers mobbed.

While the horrified townspeople watched, the dark-uniformed men began to strip the shelves, carrying all supplies out to the trucks. As the appalling task continued, the Commander of the Black Troops in the square pulled documents from his tunic, read in a booming voice.

"By special order of the Federal Health Commissioner, and in the name of the welfare of the Nation, the village of Faber is declared to be under absolute quarantine. No man, woman, or child may leave or enter it until the lifting of the quarantine, under sufferance of heavy penalty. All residents of the village of Faber are hereby warned that all attempts to violate this regulation will be dealt with summarily and drastically!"

Stunned, glancing bewilderedly at the trucks being loaded with provisions, the men and women of Faber listened to a second pronouncement:

"By special order of the Governor of this State, and for the welfare of the commonwealth, martial law is declared in effect in the village of Faber. That complete control of the government, industry, judiciary, transport, police and fire units of Faber is herewith declared to be the office of Captain Tarlaw of the Special Health Corps of the United States Government!"

FROM THE crowd a woman's voice cried in dismay. "But why are those men raiding the stores?"

The answer came in a third booming pronouncement:

"By special order of the Federal Health Commissioner, by virtue of the power vested in him by the Presidential Proclamation, by reason of the information that the germs of the plague are being spread through certain foods, it is hereby ordered that all edibles within the town of Faber be confiscated at once by the Special Health Corps and destroyed!

"It is further decreed that, since the germs of the plague may be spread by the municipal water supply, said water supply shall be completely cut off from all homes!

"To these orders I have set my hand—"

"But we'll go hungry!" The dismayed declaration came from

one of the men at the front of the anxious, motionless crowd. "If no one can enter this village—how can we get more food? Where will it come from? Those orders mean starvation for us all!"

The Black Commander snarled. "I advise you not to attempt to violate these pronouncements! Where you'll get food is your concern, not mine! You may starve, but you'll obey these commands!"

At the side of the green, the Black Troopers were still hurriedly loading their trucks. Confiscation was robbing the townspeople of their only food supply. No edible shred was being left behind.

"By God, I'll stop 'em!" one of the men declared desperately. "I've got a gun and bullets. I'll—"

"Don't! They'll kill you!"

The Commander of the Black Troops barked an order. "Go back to your homes! There will be no assembly in this village while the plague rages! Leave this green and return to your houses—or you'll go at the points of bayonets!"

When the crowd still hesitated, the Commander ordered his Black Troopers to fix bayonets, spread in skirmish formation. They began to advance across the green, and before that gleaming steel the men and women of Faber retreated. Then they scattered, running into the streets, flinging back terrified glances at the black soldiers of terror, at the emptied stores, the loaded trucks.

"Look! *Look!*"

At the edge of the green a figure had appeared. It was at first only a ghostly outline in the gloom. It materialized into a being completely enveloped in a flowing black robe, its head hooded in black. With swift steps, his eyes shining brightly through the holes in his mask, the robed man strode toward the Commander of the Black Troops. His costume bore a mark, on the center of the forehead—a gleaming white death's-head!

Through the scattering crowd a whisper ran—a whisper of mounting hope.

"The Sentinels! The Sentinels!"

As the black figure advanced, an order rang from the Commander. Instantly the Troopers whirled, leveling their rifles at the ghostly man. Facing the officer he paused, and his voice rang muffledly through his hood.

"Captain, you are acting on orders of President Young. He has determined to torture these good people with privation because they have defied him. It is another move in his plans of terrorism to wipe out all opposition and make his dictatorship absolute. It is an act which the Secret Sentinels cannot tolerate!"

THE COMMANDER'S face had paled. An icy hand was clutching at his throat—the grip of fear, his own weapon. He had been warned of the mysterious, fearless bands of black-robed men who had appeared all over the country, who constituted the greatest danger to the despotic reign of President Young. He had orders—orders in his pocket—to shoot them on sight. Yet the dark eyes flashing at him through the hood chilled him with a strange paralysis, kept him silent.

They were the eyes of Operator 5.

"You have exactly one minute, Captain, in which to tear up

your damnable pronouncements and order your troops out of this village!"

The officer straightened defiantly. He glanced at his men, who were formed in a half-circle, their rifles leveled at the black figure. The sight bolstered his shaken nerves. Suddenly he boomed a command:

"This man is an enemy of the United States government! Shoot him down!"

Instantly the man in the black robe gave a shrill whistle. The sharp sound came before the amazed Black Troopers could draw back the bolts of their rifles. As swiftly a cry burst through the night—a surge of sound that swelled from all around the green. Out from between the houses, into the light of the streets, rushed many black figures.

All were hooded! All were armed! All bore the mark of the white death's-head!

From their rifles flame spat. Across the green, bullets screamed. The attack came so swiftly that no missile left the weapons of the Black Troopers before the black-masked leader whirled away into deep shadow. From the flowing robe he jerked an automatic, fired it swiftly over the head of the Commander. And the peaceful green of Faber became a battleground!

Terror struck into the ranks of the Black Troops. They found themselves surrounded by the ghostly robed figures. Bullets splatted at them from all sides. The shrieks of their Commanding Officer, to attack, went unheeded. The Secret Sentinels advanced, a hooded army, blasting pandemonium into the ranks of the hated troopers.

Before their numbers the troops of terror retreated. The blasting of rifles echoed back from the hills as the Sentinels advanced. Into the highways, lashed with bullets, fled the soldiers of fear. Far into the open country, until they were scattered and routed, the hooded army drove them. The devastating attack ceased only in the distance and the dark.

The black rescuers, too, vanished back into the depths of the night—all save one. He had bounded to the center of the green as it cleared. Now he called through his mask to the townsmen huddling in the darkness of their yards.

"Rally to the ranks of the Secret Sentinels! Maintain martial law under your own command! Fight the tyrant Young while you are still able to fight! Wait for the signal that will sound through the air—then strike!"

At the side of the green stood the great trucks, loaded with foodstuffs—and abandoned by the retreating Black Troopers. The power of the dread pronouncements had been torn to shreds by the attack of the Secret Sentinels. The leader of the secret army, a black shadow on the green, called again his battle cry:

"Await the signal—then strike!"

As suddenly as he had appeared, he vanished back into the night.

OVER FORT CLIPSON, United States Army post in New York State, lay the quiet of midnight. Men on sentry duty at the gates paced back and forth in the darkness. No light shone over all the field. But under cover of the gloom, there was movement—the furtive movements of ghostly figures.

They issued from the barracks, darted across the fields like black phantoms—hooded, marked by the white death's-head. Their numbers grew as, silently, one after another materialized. They studied each other's eyes through their masks—bright, grim, determined eyes. Among them a whisper passed:

"The Chief Sentinel is coming tonight! The Chief is coming!"

A flutter of movement in the dark startled them; they hushed. A dark figure approached, stepping quickly. They parted, and he strode into their circle. The mark of his mask was different from theirs in only one particular. The forehead of the death's-head was emblazoned with a red number—5.

The others stood silent, alert, intent on his every word.

"Our moment is coming! Are you ready?"

"We are ready!" came the chorused answer.

The eyes of Operator 5 searched the hooded men. "Among you is one who was your Commanding Officer?"

A robed figure stepped forward. "I was formerly the Commander of this post, sir. Special orders demoted me to Second Lieutenant and stationed me on my own field—an act without precedent in military history. The present Commanding Officer is one raised from the ranks by special order of the Commander-in-Chief."

"These men," Operator 5 asked quietly, "are completely loyal to you?"

"They are, sir!"

"You realize—" the eyes of Jimmy Christopher grew sharper—"that the actions of all of you will constitute gross insubordination and mutiny? You realize that, if our attempt fails, you will be court-martialed and shot—every one of you—by a firing squad? Are you ready, in spite of that, to rebel against your own officers when the command is given?"

"We are!"

"The moment is coming! Return now to your barracks! Await the signal—then strike!"

IN THE library of his sumptuous home on upper Fifth Avenue, in New York City, sat a man of impressive bearing. J. Hudson Willing, banker of international repute, industrialist, philanthropist, was one of the most highly esteemed men in American public life. He had donated vast fortunes to innumerable charities; had undertaken social reforms of lasting benefit to the people; had endowed colleges, public libraries, playgrounds. He had razed disease-ridden slums, erected modern apartment buildings, opened them to the poor under the non-profit management of the city. He was a close personal friend of the ex-President; his name was beloved from coast to coast.

He looked up from his book when a disturbance sounded at the entrance. The doorbell had rung; Matthews, a boyhood friend who now served him as secretary, answered the summons. Loud voices carried from the hallway and brought J. Hudson Willing to his feet.

"Stand aside!"

The sound of a blow followed—knuckles cracked against flesh. Willing strode to the door and stopped in amazement when Matthews appeared. The secretary's face was trickling blood. His eyes were shining with terror. He was about to blurt out a warning when two other men appeared in the doorway— men in plainclothes, with brutal faces and glittering eyes. They fastened hands on the secretary, dragged him back, thrust him sprawling across the hall.

J. Hudson Willing turned, white-faced, and snatched up the telephone. One of the two men who had entered strode after him.

"Calling the police, Mr. Willing? You don't need to bother. We're the police!"

Willing straightened in dismay. "You're the—?"

"We're the police, and you're under arrest!"

The great man peered, stunned, at the doorway. Two other plainclothes men had appeared, whose faces were as cruel as those of the preceding pair. They held guns in their hands. Their eyes offered threats. Their manner warned against protest.

Willing's powerful face hardened as he replaced the telephone and stood so as to confront the two squarely.

"I am under arrest? Why?"

"For certain violations of strict regulations of the War-Time Banking Code established by the Federal Bank Commissioner. If you want the details—"

The speaker slipped a document from his pocket and read rapidly. Willing listened with growing amazement, rising indignation. Though his anger was rigidly controlled, he interrupted.

"That's false! In spite of the fact that I bitterly oppose this new code, I have obeyed it to the letter. You cannot find proof of a single instance of violation in any of my banks. These are trumped-up charges!"

Inexorably the secret police official continued to read. " '... The said J. Hudson Willing, by the aforementioned acts committed in violation of Federal Statute, having declared himself an enemy of the United States Government in time of war, sentence is herewith pronounced upon him by special executive order of the President of the United States.'"

"Sentence?" Willing demanded, aghast. "A sentence without trial? Impossible! Legal procedure—"

"There is no law except the word of the man whose name is signed to this document—President Young!" the officer snapped. " 'Now, therefore, by reason of his being an undesirable resident, and dangerous to the welfare of the United States, the said J. Hudson Willing will suffer himself to be transported to Midway Island in a condition of permanent exile.'"

WILLING STOOD stunned. The secret police officer, smirking with triumph, demanded: "You're a traveled man, aren't you, Mr. Willing? Perhaps, then, you know where Midway Island is located. Perhaps you appreciate—"

"I know—yes! God, this thing isn't possible! Exile—I? This is condemning me to slow death in a place I can never hope to leave!" *

The officer's smirk tightened. "You're starting for Midway right now! I have further orders here—but you'll have plenty of

---

* AUTHOR'S NOTE: Midway Island, a small coral formation, part of the Hawaiian chain and the property of the United States, is located in the center of the Pacific Ocean, 1,000 miles from Honolulu, which is itself 2,000 miles from San Francisco. This is the site of a cable station, the only other island near it being completely uninhabited. It would be difficult to find a more remote possession of the United States.

time to read them when you're on that island in the center of the Pacific. The first declares that your citizenship is revoked, that you are no longer a citizen of the United States—"

" 'No longer—!' "

"The second is a Presidential edict by which all your property of whatever character—this home, your real-estate holdings, your personal fortune, everything you own—is herewith confiscated as alien holdings and is now the property of the United States Government!"

The great man stood pale, stricken, unable to speak.

Toward him the others advanced with drawn guns. They prodded him away from his desk, through the door; forced him to the entrance. When Matthews, having heard the appalling edicts, attempted to reach his side, a swift gun-blow toppled the secretary to the floor, unconscious. Willing was forced across the sidewalk toward a waiting car.

With startling suddenness, a voice rang out from the shadow of the broad stone stoop.

"Gentlemen, step back!"

The four secret police whirled in surprise. They glimpsed a dark figure outlined against the whiteness of the stone wall—a ghostly being clad in black robe and cowl. They saw the mark of a white death's-head on the hood, a red 5 emblazoned on its forehead—and an automatic in the robed figure's hand.

"Step away from Mr. Willing! Instantly, or—"

The leader of the secret police whirled with a snarl, and his gun spat. The black figure leaped at the same instant, and the automatic in the black-gloved hand flashed flame. The shots were a signal which materialized, as if by magic, six robed figures out of the darkness along the street.

Shots rang swiftly from the guns in the hands of the Sentinels, scattering the terrified secret policemen. At the first burst, Operator 5 leaped across the sidewalk to the bewildered Willing. He jerked open the door of the waiting car; his command urged the financier into it. He looked back, and his gun flashed once at the scattering terrorists of President Young.

He slipped behind the wheel; sent the car spurting away from the curb, around the corner. While Willing sat dismayed and speechless, Jimmy Christopher sped to the east side of Manhattan.

Sharply he swung into a side street, through which a wet wind from the East River soughed. He slipped from the wheel, speaking briskly.

"Take it, Mr. Willing! You were to be deported because you fought Young's election, because he considers you a dangerous foe, because he covets your fortune. You must keep out of sight at all costs. Now follow my orders strictly, to the letter!

"Drive to the address written on this slip. You will be received without question, and you are to ask no questions. Further orders will come from me when the moment is ripe, and at that moment I will ask your help to remove Young from the dictatorship of the United States. Do you understand?"

"Yes! I will obey!"

"You must! Otherwise it means your certain death at the hands of Young's secret police!"

J. Hudson Willing gazed in amazement at the robed figure.

Operator 5 darted across the sidewalk, vanished in a deep shadow. For a moment, the great man peered into the gloom. Then he drove on.

A DARK ghost had slipped into the shadow of the bleak building flanking the East River: Operator 5 stepped out of it. He carried a briefcase. It contained the black robe of the Secret Sentinels—a robe which, to be discovered in by the secret police, would mean his certain death. He noted that the car in which he had left J. Hudson Willing had vanished: the financier was following orders. Briskly, eyes alert, Operator 5 walked west.

When he approached the door of a staid apartment house, in the East Sixties, off Fifth Avenue—only a few blocks from the raided home of the great financier—the doorman greeted him with a "Good evening, Mr. Walsh." An elevator carried him to the eleventh floor where he unlocked, with a key which had no duplicate, a door of steel covered with mahogany veneer.

He paused to glance at several newspapers which had been left on the table by the maid—a maid who had never seen Mr. Walsh, had never found his bed slept in. The obvious pro-Young flavor of every news report, he noted, and he knew that they reflected the work of the President's propagandists. There were statements that prosperity was rapidly returning; he knew they were grossly exaggerated—so much bait for the credulous. In all the printed items, Operator 5 saw quickly, there was no word of unvarnished truth—no hint of the fact that President Young was putting into action the destructive philosophies of foreign dictators.*

Operator 5—or Huntley Walsh—stepped into the adjoining bedroom, and swung toward the window a strange contrivance which sat on an anchored table. It consisted of a drum around which a rope ladder was wound; a ratchet; a powerful electric motor; and a flexible gooseneck to the end of which was affixed a camera-like black box, its lens protruding from one end. He opened the window, uncoiled forty feet of rope from the drum and dangled it outside, then pushed the black box out over the sill.

With sure movements he swung onto the ladder, lowered himself into the dark space of a passageway. He pendulumed to a small balcony on the adjacent building and brought his flashlight from his pocket. The gleam struck the lens of the black box above; uncannily, as a result of the activation of a photoelectric cell and relay, the rope ladder coiled up out of sight and the window slid shut.

Operator 5 passed through a dark apartment, into a hallway; rounded a bend in the corridor and pressed a button inscribed *Carleton Victor.* The door was opened by a cool-faced manservant who bowed with great dignity and said:

---

* AUTHOR'S NOTE: "Democracy is the system of stupidity, cowardice, weakness and half-heartedness."—Adolph Hitler.

"The dictatorship of the proletariat is nothing else than power based upon force and limited by nothing—by no kind of law and absolutely no rule."—Lenin, *Complete Works*, Volume, XVIII, page 361.

"Good evening, Mr. Victor. I'm delighted to see you back, sir."

Victor stepped in, saying: "I have been away a great deal, haven't I, Crowe? Has anything of interest happened during my absence?"

THE IMPECCABLE manservant, gentleman's gentleman extraordinaire, did not dream that the identity of Carleton Victor was a convenient mask for the activities of America's undercover ace—or for the man who was now the mysterious leader of the hooded bands known as the Secret Sentinels. Crowe believed Carleton Victor to be what he seemed—a highly proficient artist with the camera who maintained sumptuous studios on Fifth Avenue. Victor, he knew, was a photo-portraitist without a peer, for whose plates world dignitaries, industrial leaders, members of the peerage, and the famous in all fields gladly sat. His signature on a portrait was a credential of importance. He was, to Crowe, the greatest artist in the world.

Crowe considered carefully his answer to Victor's question. "As to anything important having happened, sir—you see, sir, I never read the newspapers."

"You do not know, Crowe," Victor asked in amazement, "that a new President has been elected, that he has declared the country in a state of war, and that he is building a dictatorship, hour by hour?"

Crowe blinked. "Perhaps, sir, that accounts for several strange things which have occurred—though I hadn't heard of it, sir—no, sir. In making my purchases today, sir—your favorite wine, sir, and the *filets* and the caviar—I was told that henceforth I must have—a ration card, sir. It seems that I shall be unable to buy any food without this special card."

"Indeed?" Victor inquired—and Crowe did not see the steely glint that came into his eyes.

"I inquired as to where I could obtain a card, sir, and went there. I was told most rudely that I must either pay a huge sum for it, sir—something like one thousand dollars—or sign a document. It seemed a strange sort of document, sir. It appeared to be a sort of a ballot. I have never voted, sir, of course—but this was, I'm sure, a ballot, with the name already marked on it. The name of—let me see, sir. Oh yes—Young."

"I see," Victor said quietly. "A vote to be held and stuffed into the ballot boxes at the next election in order to insure Young's reelection in spite of all else. With that device, Crowe, he will be able to rule the country as dictator as long as he lives!"

"Will he, sir?" Crowe asked. "And who, may I inquire, sir, *is* this person Young?"

Victor suppressed a grim smile. "You may count yourself fortunate, Crowe, that you do not know."

He strode to his desk, at the side of the modernistic living room of this penthouse apartment. Several newspapers lay on it. The topmost bore the strange caption of *The Secret Sentinel* and the symbol of a death's-head. With cold satisfaction, Victor read the headlines.

YOUNG'S "BALANCED" BUDGET DELIBERATELY FALSIFIED!

TREASURY LOOTED BY VAST PATRONAGE SYSTEM!

DEFENSES WEAKENED BY LACK OF SUPPORT

WHILE YOUNG USURPS PUBLIC FUNDS!
NATION MADE VULNERABLE TO ATTACK AS
RESULT OF YOUNG'S GIGANTIC STEALS!

Crowe bowed apologetically. "It is apparently a new paper, sir—which was brought to the door. I haven't read it, of course, sir, but a remarkable thing happened in connection with it. The young man who left it, as he turned away, was seized by two others. They leaped upon him, beat him, and dragged him away unconscious. A most extraordinary proceeding, sir. I heard one of our neighbors say something about the secret police being responsible."

VICTOR LISTENED grimly. The huge radio in the room was playing at low volume, with exquisite tone, and its music absorbed Crowe's attention for a moment. The manservant blinked with annoyance as the smooth strains became blurred.

"That is another odd thing, sir. I like to play the radio, sir, but of course I listen to only the best classical music. Recently there have been annoying interruptions of the programs. A lovely rendition will be begun, and suddenly a loud voice bursts out of the machine. It is impossible to avoid, sir—all over the dial. I think I shall complain to the proper authorities."

"I believe, Crowe," Victor answered quietly, "your complaint is quite unnecessary. What does this strange voice say?"

"It—there, sir! It's speaking now!"

Into the room the loud tones boomed with startling power. The musical program was completely blanketed by the fervent ring of the voice. It declared:

"The Sentinels speak! They tell you that the despot Young

once more spreads lies among you! He promised you lower taxes—and already he has increased them, adding to your burdens in order to fill his own pockets! He promised every man a job—yet the army of unemployed grows while he pays patronage to his evil supporters! He promised you prosperity— and he is stripping you of your jobs, your homes, your freedom, one by one! We will present proof of every statement we make! Listen—for the approaching hour when we will strike!"

Carleton Victor's eyes shone brightly as Crowe strode to the radio. He recognized the voice of ex-Operator Q-6—John Christopher. The voice vanished when Crowe snapped the radio switch. The manservant observed:

"Most annoying, sir!"

The sounding buzzer took Crowe to the door. Victor watched as it opened. The man who stepped in—hatless, his face pale and drawn—was J. Hudson Willing. Carleton Victor strode to him with outstretched hand.

"Good evening, Mr. Willing!" The confused financier accepted the greeting silently. "I've been expecting you—I'm delighted to see you. I'm sorry that I must leave immediately, but Crowe will take care of your every need."

Victor slipped an envelope from his pocket and passed it to the bewildered caller.

"Crowe, Mr. Willing is to be my guest for an indefinite period. See that he is made comfortable."

Willing managed a confused "Thank you!" Crowe bowed his "Of course, sir!" Victor conducted Willing to a chair; the exhausted man sank into it. Briskly, the photo-portraitist strode to the door. Crowe opened it for him, bowed again.

"When may I expect you back, sir?"

"I suggest, Crowe, that you don't expect me at all."

The manservant's eyebrows arched.

"Furthermore, Crowe—" Victor whispered it—"I urge the utmost discretion upon you. Allow no one to discover that this man is my guest—absolutely no one. Guard him carefully against visitors. If you do not, Crowe, you may be surprised to find yourself seized by the Cheka. You will be stood in front of a stone wall, Crowe, for harboring an alien enemy—and shot… Good night."

Crowe stared at the door as it closed. He turned uncertainly to gaze at Victor's amazing guest. Willing had ripped open the envelope. He was already reading its message:

> The Secret Sentinels learned of your danger and immediately took steps to protect you as one of the most important citizens of the country. We ask your help. When orders come to you, follow them strictly and without question.

To the message a number-signature, 5, was appended.

Willing gazed up to find the white-faced Crowe peering at him.

"I beg your pardon, sir!" the manservant exclaimed. "Did I understand Mr. Victor correctly? Did he say—*shot?*"

CHAPTER 10
ORDERS TO RAID

THE DARK-FACED, sharp-eyed man who strode toward the surly sentries at the gate of the White House was, to all appearances, Lieutenant Doman, of the secret police. His displayed credentials admitted him. Again, at the door of the historic edifice, he showed his countersigned card; entered. He strode directly to the door of the President's study.

Two of Young's special guards barred his way. When, once more, he proffered his credentials, the guard who took the card frowned and said:

"The President is not here."

"Then I will wait," Operator 5 answered in a disguised voice. "I have information of the highest importance for him. I can give it to no one else."

The guard, still frowning, conducted him down the hall to an anteroom. Operator 5 stepped into it, and the door closed behind him. He found himself alone. He listened alertly. As he stood there, motionless, every sense sharpened.

Operator 5 had known, because he had been on watch, that President Young was not in the White House. He had chosen his time carefully. He had entered the historic, desecrated dwelling for a secret purpose—upon an errand as dangerous as any he had ever undertaken.

He turned quickly to a connecting door, listened through it. Beyond, he knew, lay the President's study—the room from which Young had issued decree after drastic decree, each a blow at the foundations of the established Government. He heard no sound from it. It was empty.

Operator 5 found the connecting door fastened. He drew his pack of master-keys into his hand, worked carefully, deftly, at the lock. His fourth attempt drew back the bolt. With swift step he opened the door, passed through. Again he paused, listening, wary, knowing that his move, if discovered, would throw fatal suspicion upon him.

With quiet step, he crossed the room to a safe which sat in the corner behind the executive desk. It bore the name of Ursus Young. Jimmy Christopher kneeled before it and found it locked. Tensely he brought from his pocket a small, hard rubber horn to which electric cords were connected. He took out two small, black, pear-shaped objects, and inserted them into his ears. The wires which led from them connected to small but powerful batteries in his pocket. Quickly he worked.

He turned the dial of the safe, and the super-sensitive microphone unit inside the little black horn amplified a thousandfold the grinding of the safe tumblers. When he heard a click, he turned the dial in the reverse direction. With the utmost care he sought to solve the secret of the combination.

He realized that at any moment one of Young's secretaries might enter, one of the guards might open the door and see him. The phone-plugs in his ears shut away all sounds in the study itself, magnified enormously the danger he faced. With every passing second constituting an added threat, he worked swiftly....

Twice more he heard clicks as the tumblers of the lock mechanism fell into their sockets. He turned the handle of the door, his breath beating hotly, and opened the safe.

Quickly he began an examination of its contents. His eyes searched ledgers containing intricate cross-entries, long lists, reports, annotated documents which filled him with cold amazement. Some he slipped rapidly into his pockets. At last, he rose, closed the safe and spun the combination.

He returned to the connecting door, restoring the microphone instrument to his pocket; stepped into the anteroom, where he again brought his master-keys into play. Even as he withdrew the implement from the socket, he heard a sound behind him and whirled. A knob rattled; the door opened. The member of the secret police who stepped in discovered Lieutenant Doman sitting idly in a chair.

THE MAN who entered said: "I've just telephoned Headquarters. The President said he was going there, and I told him you were here. He orders you to bring your important information to him as fast as you can get there—to the former Intelligence Headquarters."

"I will go at once!"

Operator 5 strode into the hallway, the guard dogging his steps, and out of the White House. Once past the guards, free of their searching eyes, he breathed more easily. His blood pounded with cold determination as he slipped behind the wheel of a car assigned to him by Captain Critz, the merciless Commander of the secret police. His purpose in entering the White House had succeeded—yet he was obliged now to follow orders of the President and report to the offices once known as WDC-13.

He left the car, strode into the steamy restaurant which masked the approach to the secret Headquarters, and with the proper password took his way past the sentries. A secret door admitted him to a hidden elevator; the cage carried him to a higher level. His lips tightened grimly as he strode to the door of the office which once had been that of Z-7, and was now controlled by the terrorists of President Young. As he turned the knob he heard the booming voice of the man who had made himself dictator of a nation.

"You'll get results! By God, you'll get results, or you'll pay with your lives—every one of you!"

A sentry passed in word that Lieutenant Doman had arrived, and Operator 5 stepped into the office. Around the desk of Z-7, white-faced men stood; the chief officers of the terroristic Cheka. They were obviously chilled with fear as they faced the wrath of President Young. The huge man confronted them with clenched fists, eyes blazing furiously.

He whirled as Jimmy Christopher entered. "Well? What's your information, Doman?"

"I believe, sir, that the enemy known as Operator 5 is still in Washington, in hiding. I saw a man who resembled him, and trailed him, but he eluded me."

Young snarled. "Well? Where is he? Where does he hide? Did you learn that?"

"No, sir!"

A thunderous bellow of wrath broke from the President's lips. "Next time you see anyone resembling Operator 5, don't tail him—shoot him down on the spot! He is in the city—I know that! He has outwitted you all! You've failed at your most important job! I'm going to give you men one more chance to get results, and if you don't—!"

Young's great fist crashed to the desk, and the faces of the men in the office grew even whiter.

"Every night for weeks a radio station has been broadcasting sedition—and you haven't located it! It's turning this country against me—and it keeps on operating in spite of you! Why haven't you found it? Why?"

"Mr. President!" Captain Critz blurted his answer. "We have made use, repeatedly, of every scientific device. We've used the directional finders of the Navy and plotted the position of this wildcat wireless station again and again. It's never twice at the same place! It can't be a mobile station because it's too powerful—it must be in one certain location. Yet that place wanders all over the map, according to the direction-finders! We go to the spot where the lines converge—and there's no station there!"

Again Young snarled. "Failure!" He snatched a newspaper off the desk—a copy of *The Secret Sentinel*. "This filthy sheet! It's all over the country! You've only been able to find a few of the men who distribute it—you haven't at all located the plant! This dirty rag is breeding a revolution against me, and you haven't stopped it! Listen, you men! For incompetents such as you, I am bringing an old weapon of execution back into this country—the guillotine!"

Young's fist swept the air and the threatened men winced.

"By God, I'll have your heads! Your heads will roll on the

ground if you don't get results and get them fast! Do you understand that?"

Abject fear stilled the lips of every man in the secret Headquarters. A door opened during the chill pause that followed, and two men stepped into the room—officers of the American Cheka.

Young glared at them. "Well?"

One of them swallowed hard and advanced with a document.

"Reporting, to you, orders carried out, sir. The enemy known as T-3, once of the United States Intelligence, has been duly executed."

THE WORDS struck Operator 5 cold. His fists went hard at his sides. A powerful impulse seized him—to jerk out his gun and shoot down the hated despot on the spot. He had to summon every ounce of his will to repress the furious urge, to maintain the disguise T-3 had died in helping to perfect. Rigid, his heart like ice, Jimmy Christopher peered at the dictator Young.

"Good!" the President snarled. "I'll no longer waste bullets on these filthy dogs! I'll keep the blade of that guillotine bloody and sharp—if there's time to sharpen it between beheadings! Failures, all of you! I warn you, all incompetents will die!

"This band of sneaking revolutionists known as the Secret Sentinels! Who leads them? Where is their Headquarters? I've ordered you to stamp them out, to kill everyone, and instead they keep growing! Unless you find—"

The second man who had entered the office dared to interrupt in a ringing voice.

"Mr. President, I believe I have found the secret Headquarters of the Secret Sentinels!"

Suddenly Operator 5's blood rushed hot. The words were so startling, so unexpected, that he doubted his ears. He scarcely heard Young's bellowed "What?" He watched the officer of the secret police step forward and salute.

"It is in my district, sir. I've seen men slipping in and out at night. It has been extremely suspicious. It's a big warehouse building, sir, located at the corners of Gettysburg and Bunker Hill Streets. I'm positive that it's the Headquarters of the Secret Sentinels!"

Jimmy Christopher's breath locked burningly in his lungs as he peered at Young. The huge man straightened. His face gleamed with evil triumph.

"At last! Captain Critz! Call your men together at once! A hundred of them! Arm them with machine guns, dynamite, poison gas! Break into that building—raid it! Shoot down anyone you find inside it—shoot them down in their tracks! Now! Wipe that Headquarters out of existence *now!*"

"Yes, sir!"

President Young whirled on his heel and marched heavily from the inner office. While Jimmy Christopher watched, dazedly, Captain Critz of the secret police strode into the Operations Room. The others followed; the door closed as Critz's harsh voice snapped orders.

"Call all cars and sub-offices! Special orders! By God, we'll clean that building out within half an hour! We'll mow down every man inside and tear the place brick from brick!"

Operator 5's mind raced. In that secret Headquarters there were now—how many men? How many loyal Sentinels on secret duty, to be trapped and murdered by Young's terrorists? In it was the ingenious microphone system devised by Z-7, one of its wires connected to a super-sensitive device concealed in the ceiling of this room. But was that one wire, among scores, operating at this moment? Impossible to know!

Operator 5's heart sped with the cold determination that at all costs Z-7 must be warned.

IN THE Communications Room the voice of Captain Critz was crackling. Orders were being rattled into a broadcasting microphone. In Washington, continually on the prowl, were scores of cars equipped with sensitive receivers to pick up orders from the ether—cars manned by merciless secret police. Scattered throughout the city were hidden Sub-headquarters, also equipped with receivers which were never still—stations from which scores of other secret police would rush to surround the hidden Headquarters of the Secret Sentinels. At this moment, as Operator 5 listened to Captain Critz's rasping voice, the dread orders were flashing!

Operator 5 determined unhesitatingly upon a daring move. He stepped to the desk of Captain Critz, took up the telephone. When the switchboard attendant in the Communications Room answered, he said crisply: "Clear an outside line! Special orders to supplement Captain Critz's!" He heard the connection click through and when he spoke again, it was to ask for the secret number of the Sentinel's Headquarters.

A voice answered at once—the voice of a Sentinel on duty

at the special switchboard in the hidden steel-walled rooms. Operator 5 said in a whisper: "Z-7—quick!" He waited with tightening nerves until the chesty tones of the Washington Chief came to his ears.

"Z-7! Who is on duty at the microphone switchboard? Is the WDC-13 line connected? Quick!"

"Wait!… No, it is not!"

Operator 5 groaned. "Clear Headquarters!" he ordered. "The secret police have discovered it! They are organizing a raid now—it will close down at once! For God's sake abandon that Headquarters!"

"One moment!" The Chief's voice crackled. "The line is not clear. I can scarcely hear you. How can I know your warning is valid? Who are you?"

Jimmy Christopher's hands crushed the instrument. "This is Operator 5! Do you hear me, Chief? Operator 5!"

Swiftly he replaced the telephone, strode to the outer door. With rapid strides he neared the two men standing on guard duty at the panel which opened into the concealed elevator. He reached to the concealed button, which controlled the lifting mechanism; touched it. And as he stepped back he heard a quick, high-pitched voice; saw the door through which he had just passed snap open.

The man who stared out, white-faced, was the attendant assigned to duty at the telephone switchboard of the secret police.

"Stop him! He's a traitor! I heard him say he's Operator 5!"

OPERATOR 5'S answering move came fast as lightning.

His hand flashed beneath his coat and back again, gripping his automatic. He whipped it level and fired twice, so swiftly the reports were almost one. The bullets screamed past the head of the man in the doorway. With a cry of terror, the other leaped back, slammed the door shut. Again Operator 5 fired, sending a slug splintering through the panels.

"Come through and die!"

He snapped about at the two guards in the hallway. The shrieked alarm had paralyzed them with surprise. Operator 5's moves had been so swift they had no opportunity to interfere. While the blasts of the shots still echoed in the hallway, the grinding of the elevator motor sounded behind the panels.

Jimmy Christopher fired once, swiftly, as metal twinkled in the light. His bullet slammed to the gun of the one guard. He stepped back, striking out a swift blow with his left hand at the second man, while the first sprawled back, his gun spinning from his bloodied hand. Operator 5's automatic whipped up to fire another warning slug through the door. His lightning ju-jitsu attack on the second sentry brought an explosion of hot breath and a moan, then the man toppled.

The first scrambled for his fallen gun with his left hand; and Operator 5 saw the elevator panel slide. He kicked the gun on the floor away, slashed another slug at the closed door. One leap carried him into the elevator cab. Quickly he slid the grille shut, touched the button, sent the car gliding down.

Wild shouts, rasping orders, thudding heels sounded above as the cage carried Jimmy Christopher downward. He knew that the men in the office could, by telephone and in a matter of seconds, warn the sentries below. He sprang from the cab when it stopped; slid through the secret panel which opened into the rear of the cheap restaurant.

As he hurried through a swinging door, into the space beside the counter, he heard the shrill ringing of a telephone bell, saw a secret police officer whirl to answer the summons. He reached the entrance swiftly, slipped outside, sprang to his car. Glancing back through the greasy panes he saw the secret officer racing from the telephone, jerking out a gun. He kicked the motor into action, jammed the accelerator hard, and shot into the street.

Around the nearest corner he whirled, knowing that the secret police would race after him. Immediately he swung again, then a third time, a fourth, in a desperate attempt to shake off the pursuit. Only the red sticker on his windshield—the symbol of the secret police—carried him safely past traffic officers. Even at this moment, he knew, orders were being broadcast for his capture—for his death.

Pressing the motor to the limit, Operator 5 wove his way to the great brick building which housed the Headquarters of the Secret Sentinels. He swung to the curb in the shadow of the hulking structure, sprang to the door and glanced back to see, at the far corners, cars swinging into sight. They, too, were marked with the red sticker—cars of the secret police carrying out the orders of Captain Critz to raid the building and kill anyone within it. Jimmy Christopher rapped his signal swiftly; sidled through the instant the door swung open.

To the Sentinel on duty at the entrance he gasped: "Keep that door bolted. Open it for no one! Call all our men together!"

HE SPRINTED to the elevator. He heard the snarling of motors in the street—more cars of the secret police racing to the building—as the cage carried him upward with torturous slowness. When, after an interval of agony, the platform paused at the seventh level, Operator 5 sprang out to see Z-7 and Tim Donovan hurrying out of the steel-walled offices.

"Chief! Tim! The secret police are surrounding the building this moment!"

The Irish lad hurried, wide-eyed, to Operator 5's side. Z-7's dark eyes smouldered with rage. "I had to telephone orders to as many agents as I possibly could, my boy! I had to warn them off! Scores of others I couldn't reach! Are you sure—?"

"Listen!"

From below came a crashing, hammering sound—something heavy being rammed against the door of the building. The secret police were already attempting to batter it down. In the streets, guns blasted. A sharp crashing of glass echoed through the building as window panes broke under the impact of the bullets. A loud shout went up:

"Throw in the gas bombs!"

Z-7's face went white. "They're surrounding us! I've provided a means of getting out of the building, but—wait!" He hurried back to the entrance of the suite of steel-walled offices; and Jimmy Christopher strode after him. In an inner room, Z-7 turned to the wall, raised a leaf of metal. In a cavity behind was an electric switch. He pressed it home, securely locked the leaf, and turned away.

"It lights a sign on the front of the building. I've warned all our men that if they see the sign lighted, it's a signal of danger—they are to stay away. That will save those I haven't been able to reach. Come with me! Well—God! They're turning machine guns on the windows!"

The staccato sounds vibrated sharply through the building. Bullets splintered the glass of the windows below, ripped through the tarpaper, crashed into the stored goods. As the sounds echoed and reechoed, the doors of the inner offices of the secret steel-walled suite opened and startled Sentinels hurried into sight.

"After me!" Z-7 commanded them. "Every man!"

He sped toward the waiting elevator cage. Tim Donovan kept dose to the disguised Operator 5 as the Sentinels crowded around them. Z-7 sent the great cage gliding downward. When it reached the lower levels, clouds of fumes gushed up around the men—toxic gas bombs hurled through the windows broken by the machine-gun fire. Across the lower floor bullets swept as the car glided down.

It descended to the basement level and stopped with a thump. Quickly Z-7 bore his fingers into a crack of the cage floor, pulled up a small trap door which disclosed a lever in the darkness below. He thrust at it forcibly and again threw the control-switch. While his men coughed in the stinging fumes, the platform began to descend once more. Before the startled eyes of the men appeared a gleaming steel door.

Z-7 pulled it open swiftly. "Inside!" The men crowded through, into darkness. Operator 5 and Tim Donovan remained to the last. They saw the Chief reach again through the trap in the bottom of the cab, throw the lever. He leaped through the steel door; Operator 5 and the Irish lad followed. The door clanged shut and Z-7 slid a stout steel bolt into place.

A grinding sound came from beyond.

"The elevator is going back to the basement level. No one will be able to bring it down again!" Z-7's voice sounded huskily in the darkness; the sharp snap of an electric switch followed.

The amazed men looked around to find themselves at the head of a cement-walled tunnel which angled out of sight. "This leads to a building three blocks away!" Z-7 told them. "We'll be able to slip out without being seen!"

Operator 5 heard dull, resounding crashes above. "They're breaking in, Chief! Thank God we were able to bring every man with us!"

"Thanks to your warning, my boy!" Z-7 exclaimed. "If we hadn't beaten that raid the Sentinels would have been left without a leader—our entire campaign would have fallen. Concerted action would have been impossible. Young's dictatorship would have been permanently established! My boy—"

"We have suffered a serious blow, Chief," Jimmy Christopher declared solemnly. "We have lost our Headquarters!"

CHAPTER 11
THE SIGNAL SOUNDS!

INTO THE darkness of a remote, wooded area outside the Capitol of the nation—that same night—a lone car sped. It followed a paved road, swerved onto a dirt lane. Its lights

182

clicked out and it turned again into grassy ruts. Finally it was following no road at all, merely winding its way deep into the shadows of the trees. At last it stopped, and the whisper of its motor vanished into the quiet night.

From it, three dark figures alighted—Operator 5, with Z-7 at his one side, Tim Donovan at the other. Quickly they crossed a broad clearing. At the far side they paused to listen alertly; then pushed through a wall of saplings, into an area of chaotic, outcropped rock. They sought their way into a crevice, groping through darkness.

A dim gleam appeared before them, gradually brightened. They went along an earthen-walled passage lighted by a single electric bulb. At a stout door they knocked.

A rumble sounded through it, a bolt drew back; they stepped through. The grave-faced man who seized the hands of Operator 5 and Z-7 was John Christopher.

"Son! Chief! Tim! You've come here because of a serious emergency—I can see it in your eyes!"

"We're here, Dad," Jimmy Christopher answered, "on the most important mission we've ever undertaken."

They walked rapidly across the bare room. When they again passed through a door, it was to enter a spacious cavern hollowed out of the earth.

On stout plank flooring a rotary press sat. A powerful Diesel engine was running it; from it flipped a mounting pile of copies of *The Secret Sentinel*. Men in greasy coveralls were gathering them up, tying them into bundles, preparing them for secret avenues of distribution all over the United States.

This press, this secret plant, represented long, strenuous labor on the part of the Secret Sentinels. Piece by piece the machinery had been brought into this underground room. The entrance used for the purpose had been walled up following the assembling of the plant; now no entrance existed save through the cleft Operator 5 had entered. Day after day, night after night, without let-up, the Sentinels had worked secretly to erect this weapon of attack against the dictator Young.

AS OPERATOR 5 strode past the roaring press, a door opened, and from an adjoining room a girl hurried. She was pale with nervous strain. Diane Elliot who had organized the news-gathering unit of the Sentinels, who had worked with Operator 5's system of spies to build up this newspaper which reached into every city and village, hurried to Jimmy Christopher, flung her arms around him and pressed her lips to his.

"Jimmy! It's been so long since I've seen you! I've been working night and day—I haven't gone out of this place for weeks. Is *The Secret Sentinel* everything you wanted it to be, Jimmy?"

"Good girl!" Operator 5 applauded her. "Everything I wished, and more! You've done a brave job, Di—and I hope that very soon our work will be at an end."

The girl followed him eagerly as he opened the door of another spacious cavern hollowed out of the earth. Its walls were boarded; to the panels were affixed the apparatus of a broadcasting station. In the room sounded the hum of the power plant—dynamos driven by Diesel engines. Here was the vital center of the broadcasting operations which Young's secret police had never been able to locate.

These things, too, had been brought here part by part. Sentinels had stolen hundreds of storage batteries from cars, had raided licensed stations already made into propaganda bureaus for Young, had seized the equipment and turned it to their own purposes. On a table sat the microphone into which John Christopher's voice had spoken, to be spread from coast to coast and border to border. Under the direction of the scientist Marlin this station, broadcasting the new swirl waves, of which no duplicate existed anywhere in the world, had been erected.

The scientist himself stood near a panel, adjusting a giant rheostat. He turned to grip the hand of Operator 5, and Jimmy Christopher's voice rang with gratitude.

"You have helped us immeasurably, Mr. Marlin! Beginning tonight—now!—this secret station will be put to its most vital use."

He turned to Z-7. "Chief, we are without Headquarters, without any other means of reaching the Sentinels all over the country. Unless we act, decisively and at once, our cause is lost. We can wait no longer."

The Washington Chief's face was grave. "My boy, I have had no opportunity to tell you of a report that reached me just before your warning. It is the most appalling information we have received from our men. Young, when he took the President's chair, flaunted the Constitution, as you know, and referred to it as a scrap of paper. Now he is going even further. Not content with ignoring it, he is going to wipe it out of existence. He's going to enact, by force, his New Constitution—the most threatening document in the history of the world."

Operator 5 searched Z-7's smouldering eyes as the Chief continued:

"He has called a special session of Congress. He intends to address the people over a nationwide network and read the New Constitution to them, at the same time presenting it to Congress. Laws already passed will enable him to put the New Constitution into effect almost at once. The vote by Congress and the ratification by the states will be a purely perfunctory procedure. The New Constitution will become the basis of this Government exactly when Young plans it to—unless we are able to stop him."

"And the New Constitution, Chief?"

"I have all the details here, my boy. It's a document that will establish a dictatorship more despotic than any other on earth. It will go far beyond Sovietizing the United States. Once it takes effect, Young will become the lifelong dictator of the nation— never again will there be representation or liberty or justice within these shores. When the New Constitution is erected, the United States as we know it will become a thing of the past— destroyed beyond all reclamation!"

"Then, Chief, tonight is our zero hour!"

Operator 5 turned briskly to the table on which the microphone sat. He spoke crisply to Marlin, and the scientist threw switches, adjusted knobs and indicators which placed the powerful station into full operation. Above ground, as motors went into action, balloons rose—captive balloons concealed by day among the trees. They carried up the antennae of the station.

Anxiously, Z-7, Tim Donovan and Diane Elliot watched Operator 5 as Marlin signaled readiness.

Jimmy Christopher brought the microphone close to his lips. His eyes flashed fire.

"Sentinels! Secret Sentinels of America! Our moment has come! We strike!"

There was no sound in the underground room save the ringing words of Operator 5, the faint hum of the dynamos beyond.

"Sentinels, you have your orders! Act upon them now! Begin your march! Washington is your objective! The destruction of the despot Young is your aim! The preservation of the United States of our forefathers, the salvation of the nation we love, is our paramount purpose.

"This is your signal!

"*Strike!*"

OVER THE United States, from coast to coast and from border to border, the stirring command of Operator 5 carried.

"This is your signal! Strike!"

In millions of homes, in offices, in thousands of moving cars, in lonely cabins, in desert huts, in magnificent mansions, in Army camps, aboard U.S. Naval vessels, in airplanes flying, in squalid tenements and sumptuous apartments, radios reproduced the clarion call.

"Your signal! Strike!"

Night lay over the nation when the first summons to arms sounded. Again and again, as the hours passed, the arousing words echoed. Over and over the words rang through the ether, sounding the long-awaited tocsin.

187

"Our hour has come! Strike!"

In the streets of great cities, in the lanes of scattered villages, black armies sprang into being—armies of robed and hooded men. They swarmed from the shadows to form their advancing ranks.

Squads tramped along, and more squads joined them. They carried rifles, shotguns, target pistols, automatics, revolvers, cudgels, knives—every manner of weapon human hands could reach. The magic words crying from the sky brought into existence a swelling, fearless Army of Revolution!

Grimly these masked men commandeered every movable vehicle they could find. They thrust drivers from the wheels of automobiles—drivers who feared to join them. They seized trucks, delivery wagons, motorcycles, police cars, imported limousines, private airplanes. They swarmed down rivers in any kind of boat they could find. They swooped into the railroad yards of the nation and took command of crack express trains, of freights, of hand-cars. They mobbed upon the airports, and black-hooded pilots took them aloft—if not Black Hoods, then pilots forced to fly at the points of guns. Across earth and sky, toward the focal point of the nation's Capitol, they came swarming—the cowled Army of Revolution!

"Our hour has come! Strike!"

The alarm spurred men to action on scattered fields of United States Army posts. Uniformed men shot dice with death—rose in mutiny against the incompetent, merciless officers appointed by President Young to rule them. Following the orders of Commanders once broken by the despot, they struck to reclaim the service for their Nation. And out of those fields, commanded by black-hooded officers, men came by the thousands. In Army trucks, in staff cars, in tanks, in battle planes and bombers and pursuits, they turned upon the Capitol of their own nation!

"Strike!"

Aboard the battle fleets of the Atlantic and the Pacific, squadrons of the United States Navy—began mutiny! Officers, the tools of Young, found themselves besieged by their men—men who now refused to follow their orders. The blue of the Navy was led by the black of the Secret Sentinels, and the color of blood marred glistening decks. To the helms of the fighting ships came men who had before commanded them—on the sea the strength of the Secret Sentinels took charge.

"Strike!"

ALONG A lonely road, under cover of the night, a regiment of Secret Sentinels marched. The rhythm of their hard heels mingled with the swishing of their black robes. The glitter of the varied weapons in their hands was no less bright than the glint of their eyes. Their masked faces were turned toward the east, and unflagging determination prodded them. Their ranks were broken by comrades who had seized upon cars and trucks along the way. They marched because it was their only way of advancing. The signal had sounded and they had risen—from the very heart of Young's stronghold, New Cornwall!

Their officer, sensing a movement in the darkness ahead of them, commanded: "Alert!"

Onto the road, in their path, black figures rushed from the shelters of the trees along the way. Rifles glittered in the light of a wan moon. Uniform buttons shone. The sword of a Commander flashed high to signal an order. "Ready! Fire!" The Black Troops of Young shot with merciless aim into the ranks of the Secret Sentinels.

The cowled leader of the masked men snapped a command that brought their grotesque assortment of weapons into action. The flame of gunfire lighted the road as the battle swiftly reached its height. On the lonely thoroughfare the conflict broke as desperately as in the days when the ragged Minutemen turned their flintlocks upon the trained Redcoats. And black figures fell.

The order of the cowled leader sent his men into an advance which played withering fire into the scattering ranks of the Terror Troopers. With relentless determination they pressed forward. The heavy blasts of shotguns mixed into a chorus of death with the spiteful snapping of target pistols. Blood colored the road. Sentinels dropped and lay still at the side of fallen Black Troopers as their ranks advanced. Furiously they fought, turning their guns into the trees as Young's corpsmen fled.

Their ranks thinned, their dead left behind them, some of them wounded, they reloaded their weapons and their heels beat again in dogged rhythm. The Secret Sentinels marched on!

AT ALAMO FIELD of the U.S. Army Air Corps, swift pursuit planes sat on the line. In their pits, pilots waited while radials roared. In the observation cubbies, goggled men checked their scarf-ringed machine guns. An order had rushed them from the barracks to their ships, and now an officer, marching from the Operations Office, bellowed another command into the roar of the motors.

"The Secret Sentinels are approaching Washington! Our Commander-in-Chief has ordered them stopped! Get into the air! Mow them off the roads with your machine guns!"

A fresh roar came from the radials as the pilots opened their motors. Alamo Field had been established, by a series of Presidential orders, as a stronghold of Young. The officers were his puppets. The fliers were his marionettes. No man was on the field who was not part of Young's organization of terrorists. He had swept out all officers who were not ready to obey his slightest whim, had made Alamo Field a winged unit in his organization of terror spreaders.

"Take off!"

The thunder of the motors rose to an ominous pitch, and the pilots stared across the open field ahead of them.

Suddenly they saw black phantoms appear. Suddenly, ghostly figures materialized out of the night—each figure marked with the dread symbol of the death's-head. A mass of moving black appeared, and in its midst were metallic glitters. Swiftly the attack began. Weapons flashed, bullets streamed at the planes about to slash into the air.

Deliberately the pilots turned their roaring props into the ranks of the hooded men! They sped their crates so that the tails lifted, and the barrels of their machine guns bore down toward the shadowed ranks. Sharp rat-tats stuttered death into the ranks of the Sentinels—across the sand beat the power of a terrific attack between the hooded soldiers on foot and the winged hawks of Young!

A fusillade smashed into the pit of a speeding plane, and it swerved. Its wing wiped low, ripped off. It spun into a heap of debris as its pilot spilled, riddled, from the pit.

The vicious sweep of machine-gun bullets turned with greater fury upon the Sentinel lines. A plane cut through the black ranks and howled up—to sag as a burst of slugs from the cowled men's guns wilted it in midair.

A second plane spun to its doom. A third, its pilot dead at the controls, crashed into the fence at the border of the field. The flame of bullets marked the night as the battle became a storm of flying lead—a storm which passed as quickly as it broke.

Sentinels lay dead on reddened sand. The flames piled up; burning ships lighted the bodies of the fallen. Swiftly the power of the Sentinels had struck against Young's vultures—at the cost of scores of them. But now, on the field, no motor roared, no wing moved. The devastating onslaught had broken the wings of the bloody brood. No plane could take off now to mow down the advancing Sentinels!

And over every approach to the Capitol, the Secret Sentinels were marching forward!

IN THE secret rooms which had once been Headquarters WDC-13 of the United States Intelligence—now the central office of the dread secret police of the despot Young—a fearsome tension existed.

Clattering teletype machines, crackling wireless instruments, shrilling telephones, breathless secret couriers, all piled startling report upon startling report—news of the advance of the army of the Secret Sentinels upon Washington.

Beside the desk which had once been Z-7's, President Young

stood. His great fists pounded as he rapped out orders, his face was empurpled with wrath, his snarling voice lashed like a whip at his apprehensive lieutenants. He snatched at each printed dispatch rushed from the Communications Room, and as he read them—advices that the army of insurrection was flooding swiftly nearer—his eyes flared with murderous hatred and determination.

"Those damned rebels have got to be stopped!"

"We've tried to stop them!" the Chief of the secret police protested. "We're fighting them in every way possible! We've shot them down on every road—and they keep coming! We've knocked them out of the sky—and they keep flying! They can't be stopped!"

"By God, I'll stop them!"

Young spun as the door flashed open. The man who advanced toward him, breathing hotly, was Lieutenant Cusak, one of the deadliest agents in the dread secret police. He snapped a salute, blurted:

"We've just taken two prisoners, Mr. President! One is the girl, Diane Elliot! The other is an ex-intelligence operator known as J-8."

"What!" Young straightened, a glitter of triumph in his eyes. His voice grated as he demanded: "Where are they?"

"In the outer office now, sir! We've suspected the girl of operating the seditious newspaper called the *Secret Sentinel*. We now have proof of it! I've had J-8 spotted, suspecting he was relaying information to the newspaper. I followed him today and captured him with the girl."

Young's lips curled. "Good, Cusak! Good!"

"J-8 was carrying a written report out of town when I followed him—information he had gotten somehow from the Treasury Department. I have it with me."

Cusak whipped the folded paper from his pocket, proffered it. Young snatched the paper. As he read, his face went white with fury.

"J-8 went to a meeting place he had already arranged with the girl," Cusak continued. "I saw him hand her that report. She was of course going to print it in her secret newspaper. I brought her and J-8 here."

"Bring them in!"

Young's command snapped Cusak around to the door. He jerked it open, rapped out an order which brought two other terrorist agents marching into the room. Between them walked the prisoners, held securely. Before President Young, the captives were brought to a halt.

Diane Elliot stood pale, her eyes defiant. That she had been handled roughly was evident from the disarray of her hair and clothing. Her eyes did not flinch from Young's; nor did those of Operator J-8, who stood erect at her side.

Young's thick lips curled contemptuously as he peered at them. "You are both guilty of treason," he declared harshly. "You have aided in inciting a damned band of revolutionists to an attack upon the Government of the United States. You both know the penalty for that offense—death."

Diane stood motionless, her eyes defying those of President Young. Nor did J-8 speak any word.

Young's gaze stabbed at him. "It is my order, J-8, that the sentence of death be executed upon you at once!"

J-8'S FACE went deathly white. His lips drew to a line; but still he did not speak. His hands tightened into fists when he saw President Young's acid gaze turn again upon Diane Elliot.

"It is my pleasure," the despot declared slowly, his voice edged with evil triumph, "to handle your case in a slightly different manner, Miss Elliot. My secret police have supplied me with a wealth of information concerning you. I know, for instance, that you have become very dear to Operator 5. He will stop at nothing to save you from harm. Am I right?"

Desperately Diane Elliot searched the hard eyes of Young—striving to fathom the secret of the merciless plan forming in his mind. But she made no answer.

"It is my decision," Young stated, an ugly smile curving his lips, "to stay the time of your execution, Miss Elliot, until Operator 5 himself is able to give the signal which will start the fall of the guillotine knife on your neck—if he chooses!"

Diane Elliot swayed slightly. At her side, J-8 began a step forward. In hot fury he blurted: "By God, you can't do that!" Diane Elliot's tense hand seized his wrist, stayed him.

"It's quite useless," she said quietly. "Jimmy can't be stopped now. I don't want him to stop—no matter *what* happens."

Young was peering sharply. "I believe you will find," he said raspingly, "that Operator 5 will fail when he faces the test."

His knuckles rapped the desk. "Orders! Take J-8 to the guillotine at once! Waste no time about it! Behead him! Hold the girl until I order her put beneath the knife!"

Again the hands of the two secret police forced Diane Elliot and J-8 to move. They were thrust out of the office. President Young's eyes glinted with a growing sense of victory as he turned to face the Chief of the secret police.

"As soon as that guillotine has been used to behead J-8, bring it to the lawn in front of the Capitol. Erect it there! Put the girl under the knife when the revolutionists reach the Capitol. If Operator 5 chooses to order his men to advance then, he'll do it at the cost of that girl's life!"

Again Young's knuckles clicked.

"See that this information is spread! Let it become known to the ex-Intelligence operators hiding in the city! Let them carry the word to Operator 5! See that he learns of the choice he must make—and learns it as soon as possible!"

The Chief of the secret police stared at Young in admiring fascination as the President strode from the office. When the door slammed, the Chief rapped out orders to the agents waiting in the room—orders by which the news of the President's decision would be circulated and picked up by the hidden operators of the destroyed Intelligence Service.

As the men hurried from the room, he lifted the telephone and asked quietly for a number.

"J-8," he said levelly when the connection went through, "a prisoner of state, to be executed by Presidential order, is now being taken to the site of the guillotine. Behead him at once! Immediately afterward, transfer the guillotine to the lawn in front of the Capitol. Hold it ready for the execution of a second prisoner of state, a girl—Diane Elliot."

ALONG A broad cement highway which led to the hub of the nation, black-robed men marched, their black hoods marked with the sign of the skull—Secret Sentinels. Darkness covered their movements. Through the slits of their masks they studied the road ahead intently, alert for attack. With even strides they advanced until a shouted command of their officer turned them from the road.

"Break ranks! We wait here for further orders!"

As the robed Sentinels spread into the field beside the road, a glare of light shone in the distance behind them. A swift car sped over the cement, bearing the identification mark of the white skull. When it reached the point at which the robed men had left the road, it braked to a stop. From it climbed two figures, also cloaked, but distinguished a little differently by the marks on their skull insignia.

The forehead of the white skull of one carried a red numeral 5; the other bore the cryptic designation Z-7.

The Commander of the hooded men advanced, snapped a salute. The eyes of Jimmy Christopher shone dark blue through the slits of his hood as he looked among the robed ranks.

"We are waiting for the final signal to advance, sir!"

"The final signal," Jimmy Christopher declared evenly, "will be relayed to you by radio. All our men are waiting for it now. It will go out from our car, and will be picked up by the equipment of other cars, and by airplanes. The planes will drop flares as an order to start the final advance. Our move toward the Capitol will be a concerted advance."

"Yes, sir!"

"The signal will come at any moment. Hold yourselves ready!"

Operator 5, with Z-7 at his side, began to retrace his steps to his car. But he paused, alertly, when another gleam shot along the road. Glaring headlamps flooded the road as a light sedan sped near, roaring from Washington.

It braked suddenly near the car of Operator 5. A man in plainclothes sprang from the wheel and rushed through the darkness. He brought up, breathless, before Jimmy Christopher, and saluted.

He was one of the ex-Intelligence operators who had volunteered for dangerous espionage duty in the very heart of President Young's camp of power.

"Special report, sir!" he exclaimed. "Diane Elliot and J-8 have been captured by the secret police! J-8 has already been beheaded!"

Jimmy Christopher's eyes blazed through the slits of his mask. His gloved hand shot out to grip the arm of the courier. "Did you say Diane Elliot has been captured?"

"She has, sir! She's being held prisoner now! She has been sentenced to death on the guillotine by Young!"

Jimmy Christopher peered haggardly at the masked eyes of Z-7, as if unable to believe the words he had heard. The ex-Chief's gaze was fiery.

"Are you positive of that?" he asked the messenger huskily.

"Yes, sir! Young has been using the guillotine again and again. He's had scores beheaded already publicly. It has become a worse reign of terror than the French Revolution! He's ordered the guillotine set up in front of the Capitol tonight, and he's going to order Diane Elliot beheaded there!"

OPERATOR 5 stood rigid.

"It's no secret why he's doing it, Operator 5! It is going to prevent our taking the Capitol! If you signal our men to attack, the girl will be killed. Your signal will carry our men into the Capitol—they are waiting everywhere now—but it will also cause the girl's death. Young has planned it deliberately in order to prevent your giving the signal!"

The eyes of Operator 5 grew dark with agony.

"The guillotine has already been set up in front of the Capitol! The girl is there now! Young is waiting!"

Jimmy Christopher blurted: "God, Chief!"

Z-7's hand seized his arm. "You can't give the signal at the cost of Diane's life! If you did, the success of our attack would mean nothing to you. Diane's death would haunt you the rest of your days. You can't face that, my boy!"

Operator 5 could not speak.

"For my part," Z-7 declared huskily, "I refuse to signal that girl's death! You cannot, and I will not!"

Jimmy Christopher peered unwaveringly at the ex-Chief.

"Our men are ready, Z-7," he said quietly. "They are waiting at this very moment to begin the attack. Our plan must not fail! With the very existence of the nation at stake, I can't let— Diane's life—weigh against—"

His voice failed him. Then he straightened, and a new gleam came into his darkened eyes.

"If neither you nor I can give that signal, Chief, one of our

The keen blade hissed through the air and slashed the rope held tight in the executioner's hands!

under-officers must give it. It's not possible to stop our attack now. I refuse to consider it possible. We've got to go ahead, no matter what it costs. And rather than hear the voice of another man give that signal, I choose to give it myself!"

"My boy!" Z-7 choked out the protest. "Diane means more to you—!" He broke off, stopped by the determination shining in the eyes of Jimmy Christopher.

"Chief," Operator 5 declared firmly, "perhaps there is a chance. Young will not order Diane executed as long as he is playing his game against us. Once she is—dead, the power of his plan will be gone. Until the blade of that guillotine falls, there's a gambling chance that—"

Operator 5 broke off tightly. Quickly he turned to the Commander of the detachment of robed men. "Await the signal!" he ordered.

He strode stiffly toward the heavy sedan which had brought him to the spot, and Z-7 followed him. He slipped beneath the wheel of the car, took up the microphone that was connected with the power-shortwave wireless installation. His voice was strained and husky as he spoke words which flashed to all the surrounding country.

"Sentinels, attention! Calling all officers! Keep yourselves ready! The signal for our advance will be given soon! Wait for it, and when it sounds—order your men to attack!"

Z-7 sat tensely beside Jimmy Christopher. The powerful car roared over the road toward Washington....

JIMMY CHRISTOPHER'S black-gloved hands gripped the wheel tightly as he directed the car into the center of the web of streets radiating from the Capitol building. He had pressed all possible power from the motor while on the open road. Now he saw avenues patrolled by Black Troopers; sensed in the air a tension that was about to snap. Undercover, he knew, were Sentinels waiting to begin the attack—waiting for the signal.

He turned a corner and the Capitol came into full view. None of the Black Troopers moved toward him; they were allowing him to proceed, he knew, at the orders of President Young. His black robe, the skull insignia of the insurrectionists, aroused no action on the part of the secret police who must be watching. Young, he realized, was playing the desperate game to the limit, confident that it would render Operator 5 and the Secret Sentinels powerless.

Jimmy Christopher leaned forward intently, gazing across the great open space in front of the Capitol. There, the beams of searchlights turned upon it, stood a grim machine of death—a guillotine. The sharp blade of its poised knife was a gleaming line in the glare. Near it three men stood—and a girl.

Diane Elliot, her hands tied behind her, stood outlined against the darkness, clearly visible to Jimmy Christopher as he drove closer. Her arms were held by two uniformed Black Troopers, whose faces were masked in black. Beside the dread guillotine stood the executioner—an apparition of horror, garbed in blood-red. The eyes of all of them turned full upon the car as it stopped.

Grimly Operator 5 stepped out. Z-7 came quickly to his side. They peered at the great white Capitol building behind the guillotine. Around it, ring upon ring of Black Troopers stood on guard, their officers waiting and alert to utter quick commands. The rifles of the Terror Troops glittered in the light.

Jimmy Christopher paused. At his signal, Z-7 returned to the car, and he resumed the wheel.

Carefully he cranked the windows of the sedan shut. Throwing the heavy car into gear, he sent it crawling directly toward the guillotine.

As it moved, the red-clad executioner signaled. Instantly the two masked troopers thrust Diane Elliot forward. They forced her to kneel, fixed her throat against the notched board of the machine of execution. The executioner picked up the rope connected with the trip of the weighted blade.

One jerk on that rope, Operator 5 knew, would send the keen knife slicing down through Diane Elliot's neck.

The girl looked up, her eyes shining with tears, as Operator 5 stopped the car. Her white face, her expression of pleading, brought a pinching pain to his heart.

With Z-7 again at his side, he faced the guillotine. He saw the executioner's hand move. The rope tighten….

His one gloved hand stole through a slit at the side of his robe. His fingers reached for the buckle of his belt.

One of the black-masked troopers stepped forward and spoke in a crackling voice.

"You are Operator 5. The order of the President is that this girl is to be executed—at your own signal. You have chosen to come to this spot; now, sir, you will choose whether or not to signal the fall of this knife."

Operator 5 peered up at the gleaming blade, and the sharp brightness of its edge chilled him.

"We are informed by our secret police that your bands of revolutionists are waiting outside the Capitol for your signal. You may, if you wish, give that signal to advance. When it sounds, it will bring the blade of the guillotine down."

Jimmy Christopher's gaze turned again to the face of Diane Elliot. She was striving to look up at him. She blurted in a whisper:

"Don't stop, Jimmy! Don't stop! Give the signal now!"

The black-masked officer's crackling voice sounded again. "The President's order is that the sentence of death will not be executed upon Diane Elliot—if you issue orders to your revolutionists to retreat now! Once your men act upon those orders and the danger of attack is removed from the Capitol, Miss Elliot will be released."

The girl's whisper was scarcely a breath. "Don't listen, Jimmy! Give the signal!"

"You will," the masked officer declared flatly, "decide the issue here and now!"

Operator 5 answered tightly. "Very well. I will decide the issue here and now."

Z-7'S ALERT eyes followed his deliberate move as he reached through the open door of the sedan. Operator 5 lifted out the microphone connected with the shortwave installation. The black cord trailed as he stepped close to the executioner, whose hand tightened on the rope until it was taut. The slightest of jerks, it was evident, would release the poised blade.

The masked officer addressed Operator 5 sharply: "Give your orders!"

Jimmy Christopher's voice rang clearly.

"Sentinels—attention!"

In his left hand Operator 5 held the microphone. The fingers of his right tightened upon the hilt of his concealed rapier.

He saw Z-7's hand sliding toward an automatic holstered beneath the Chief's black robe. Beyond, on the steps of the Capitol, the ringed Black Troops were ready with their rifles. Their officers were alert, waiting to snap quick orders.

The blade of the guillotine gleamed in the light; the hand of the executioner had closed hard on the release-rope. Nevertheless the voice of Operator 5 rang again into the ether:

"Calling all officers! Orders! Advance! *Attack!*"

Instantly Operator 5 dropped the microphone and whipped his rapier out through the slit in his cape. The keen blade hissed through the air, and slashed the rope held tight in the red-clad figure's hand. The executioner jerked the release—and the blade of the guillotine remained caught on the trip.

Operator 5 sprang swiftly as the executioner, recoiling, snatched at a huge automatic holstered against his red hip. The two masked officers flashed hands toward their guns.

Z-7's weapon streaked in the light as they made the move. Two shots sounded; two shrill cries followed the explosions; then Z-7 was leaping between the officers and the girl on the guillotine.

"Stay back!"

Operator 5's reclaimed rapier was lightning on the hand of

the executioner, and steel sparkled against steel. The blood-red figure recoiled again as the slashing edge struck all strength out of his hand. Jimmy Christopher brought the blade upward and instantly the steel lightning struck again. He had the needle point poised over the very heart of the executioner.

"Stay back!"

Z-7's command rang once more as he forced the two masked officers away. His bullets had accurately found their wrists, disabling them. He reached for the bound arms of Diane Elliot as Operator 5 forced the executioner away from the guillotine. Jimmy Christopher's order echoed the Chief's swiftly.

"Into the car! Quick!"

He darted back, guiding Diane toward the open door. Z-7 whirled behind the body of the sedan, leaped inside as Operator 5 darted to the wheel. The motor snarled, even as the executioner whipped his weapon up and fired twice, point-blank, at the head of Operator 5 behind the windshield. The glass turned white, splintered—but did not break. Jimmy Christopher sent the car hurtling forward.

"Fire!"

The command rang from the officers of the Black Troopers stationed around the Capitol. Instantly rifles flashed. A fusillade of shots streamed at the sedan as it gained momentum. Bullets pelted the black body, scarring it—but they did not penetrate. With Diane Elliot beside him, sobbing, clinging to his arm, Z-7 crouched behind him—all of them surrounded by bulletproof glass and armored steel—Operator 5 sped the car at its swiftest away from the Capitol.

207

Overhead, flares dropped from planes flitting like bats in the night. Over all the surrounding country the glare spread, reflecting in the grim, upraised eyes of the Sentinel Army. The signal to advance!

Again, as the motor roared, Operator 5 grimly called through the ether:

"Sentinels, attack!"

INTO THE radiating streets of the hub of the nation, the black flood of revolution poured. Thousands tramped toward the golden mark of their destination—the glittering dome of the Capitol. Countless cars choked the streets, approaching from all directions. In the air, planes roared, bringing hooded wielders of vengeance, swooping down to any field that offered a possible landing. From the railroad terminals black-robed men mobbed, abandoning the trains they had commandeered. The power of the Secret Sentinels converged upon the edifice that symbolized the despotic power of Young.

Black Troops of the President fired upon their advance—and retreated before their fury. His secret police sought to block their way by a hail of tear gas and lethal-gas bombs—but they advanced. Nor did they forget the dead who lay behind them. They came hungry, thirsting, aching with fatigue, burning with the pain of wounds, wracked with illness—but they came.

Among them moved, alertly, men organized under a carefully built plan by Operator 5. The former members of the Intelligence Service, waiting under Jimmy Christopher's command for this moment, hastened to execute the details of a strategy to control the vital points of the city.

Some hurried into the governmental buildings. A squad massed at the entrance of the secret rooms which had once been WDC-13 and trapped whatever secret police were inside. Others swiftly took control of the telephone system, the telegraph network, the master-switches of the lighting and power systems of the city.

Each move had been planned carefully in advance; each move was enacted now with precision.

Toward the broad steps of the Capitol building the black flood poured. Around the Capitol, lines of Black Troopers massed. Drilled like human machines, disciplined by cruel officers, they presented a solid front to the swarming thousands of the Secret Sentinels. Rifles bristled toward the advancing crowds of the hooded men. And upon the ringing commands of the terror leaders, those weapons spat.

Bullets smashed the lighted windows of the great Hall of Representatives where, tonight, Congress was meeting in a joint, extraordinary session, by special order of the President. Bullets scarred the white stone of the great building. Upon the steps, Black Troopers fell as they retreated before the cowled forces that could not be stopped. All around the building the storm of battle raged.

Swooping close to the white walls, the robed men cut apart and drove away the lines of the Black Troopers. To the base of the steps, under the shadow of the great gilt dome, advanced new lines of hooded men. Theirs were the skilled maneuvers of men trained in fighting. They were United States Infantrymen, wearing the black of revolution, charging in an attack upon their own Capitol!

A hail of lead drove back, to the top of the steps, the last remnant of the Black Troopers. Against the great doors, the Commander of the terror corps took his last stand.

Toward him, with majestic stride, a robed and cowled man mounted, advancing without fear of the rifles of the Black Troopers. He brought himself to a stop, facing the white-faced Commander of the corpsmen. Through the mask his voice rang firmly.

"I call upon you, sir, to surrender!"

The Commander peered in terror at the black mob on the steps, at the glittering Army rifles leveled at him. He glanced fearfully at his own broken ranks. He growled an order that caused his men to lower the muzzles of their weapons. He flung his sword wrathfully upon the stone and it rang like a death-knell to his power.

"I have no choice! I surrender!"

THE SENTINEL COMMANDER turned. A squad of his men advanced. They jerked the rifles from the hands of the cowed Black Troopers, forced the corpsmen to the side of the great portico. The way to the great door of the building was opened. The Sentinel Commander turned smartly, marched down the steps with his men clearing an aisle for him.

A car had drawn to the very base of the steps. Two others stopped behind it. Out of the first stepped a brisk-moving figure whose death's-head symbol was distinguished from all the others by the red numeral 5. Beside him appeared a man who bore the designation Z-7. A small figure accompanied them—a boy.

To the robed Operator 5, the Sentinel Commander reported: "We have taken the Capitol, sir!"

The voice was that of a man who had suffered keen humiliation and disgrace through a drastic edict of the President— Major-General Douglass, former Chief of Staff.

At Operator 5's command, the doors of the other cars were opened. From them came a group of men and women neither masked nor robed. They stepped quickly to the side of Jimmy Christopher. Foremost among them was a man, the sight of whose grave face brought gasps of surprise from the Sentinels standing near.

He was the ex-President of the United States.

Operator 5 said quietly: "Follow me!"

He strode quickly up the broad steps of the Capitol, with Z-7 at his one side, the ex-President at his other. The men and women from the cars followed.

They moved directly to the great doors of the building, the roar of the mob sounding behind them. Just outside the entrance the cowled figure marked by the red 5 turned and raised his arms in signal.

Every voice hushed. Every movement stilled. Around the embattled Capitol silence spread.

The vital moment, when the fate of a great nation had to be decided, was at hand.

CHAPTER 12
MAKERS OF DESTINY

O N THE speaker's platform of the great Hall of Representatives, a score of men—all puppets of the despot Young—were waiting. Their faces were pale, their eyes anxious. There was scarcely a movement, save that of a technician making last adjustments of the bank of microphones which sat on the rostrum. At one side another technician sat before the monitor panel of the broadcasting lines.

An extraordinary joint session of the Congress of the United States was about to begin, and the words spoken in this historic hall were to be radioed from coast to coast.

In their seats sat every Senator and Representative—silent, waiting. They had heard the turmoil outside the building; the silence that reigned now filled them with an ominous foreboding.

There was a flutter of movement as the Speaker of the House advanced to a position in front of the microphones. He had been signaled by the technicians that the lines were clear. He rapped his gavel, and the sound echoed on its way across the country—around the world.

"Order! This extraordinary joint session of the Senate and the House of Representatives of the United States, called by special proclamation of the President, is declared in session!

"I declare all preliminary business dispensed with. The President comes before you with a vital message. He addresses you now!"

A door opened behind the platform. Through it marched the hard-faced Chief Executive. His bodyguard of deaf-mutes strode at his sides. He carried a sheaf of documents in his hand. As he stepped toward the microphone, the Speaker seized his arm and whispered.

"Mr. President, they are all around us! It is impossible to tell what is happening! Look at the windows—broken by bullets! Listen—there isn't a sound! I warn you—"

"The Black Troops have driven them back—it's all over," Young declared coldly. "The nation is waiting for me to speak, and nothing is going to stop me. I have the situation under control."

He advanced to the microphones, stared out over the assembly. He saw fear in their faces—the fear by which he ruled them. His thick lips curled in an evil smile. The silence grew intense as he bent to speak words that would carry to the four corners of the country and encircle the globe.

"Members of the Senate and the House of Representatives of the United States! We face a national emergency. We are determined to handle it with courage and decisive action. When a system of government fails, a new system must be erected in its place. I propose to lay the cornerstone of a new government tonight. I propose a New Constitution to replace the old. A New Constitution to—"

Suddenly the entrance of the hall burst open. Through it rushed black-robed men, weapons glittering in their hands. Quickly they sped along the aisles, taking positions at the sides

213

of the great hall. Senators and Representatives found themselves peering into the muzzles of guns as they sat in their seats.

On the platform, Young's deaf-mutes sprang to his side. His puppet statesmen muttered exclamations of fear.

Young hesitated as black-cowled men came toward him. He whipped around to command: "Don't fire! Say nothing! The whole nation is listening in. Wait until—!" To the technician at the monitor board he snapped: "Switch off the microphones! Make some excuse!"

HE WAS too late. A hooded man with a menacing gun had already covered the technician at the board. His command was crisp and clear:

"Keep that line open!"

Another black-robed man advanced, snatched the technician out of the chair, took control of the knobs. He slipped on the earphones, quickly read the meters, made sure the microphones were still functioning.

President Young's face grew purple with wrath. None of the sentinels had moved any closer to him. They lined the walls like shadows, leveling their guns, making no sound. Senators and Representatives, attempting to rise and flee, had been forced back into their seats by the cowled sentries; yet no suggestion of disturbance had reached the microphones. Desperately Young determined upon bravado. As though nothing untoward had occurred, he leaned forward and resumed his speech.

"I propose a New Constitution, gentlemen, which will remake a futile government into one of lasting power and—"

He paused in dismay again, as a commanding black figure

appeared at the head of the aisle—a cowled man marked with the white death's-head and the red figure 5. A second, designated Z-7, came to the first one's side. Between them stood the ex-President of the United States; behind them were men and women, unmasked, their faces solemn. Quickly, with sure steps, they strode down the aisle to the platform.

Young's deaf-mutes closed around him. Their guns gave not the slightest pause to the approaching Commanders of the Sentinels. Operator 5 strode upon the platform; Z-7 followed him. They faced President Young.

Young had ceased speaking; his face was deathly white. He turned, as if to command his bodyguard to shoot—and the ringing voice of Operator 5 stopped his move at its beginning.

"President Young! The entire nation, the whole world, is listening to us here. The microphones on that table are still alive. Secret Sentinels have taken command of the entire broadcasting system. They are stationed along the main line, in the key stations, at the relays stretched across the country, at the controls of every broadcasting unit in the United States. Whatever is said here, whatever sound is made, will reach the ears of the millions you have victimized with your terrorism!"

Young retreated from the microphones. He snarled at his bodyguards: "Take him away!"

The deaf-mutes saw his lips work; glanced around at the hooded men whose guns were leveled at them.

They made no move. Fear chilled them. They took retreating steps as Jimmy Christopher stepped closer to Young.

"Until I choose to give the signal, the coast-to-coast broadcasting system will keep this scene open to the world. I warn you, Mr. President, that this Capitol, as well as every vital point in the United States, is at this moment under the complete control of the Secret Sentinels.

"We have taken command of the Army from coast to coast. The entire Navy is under our orders. At this moment our infantry rule the Capitol; six battleships lie off this coast with their big guns trained on the dome of this building. Your dummy General Staff are being held prisoners in their consultation room by the Sentinels. Your terroristic secret police are completely overwhelmed."

Young bellowed: "This is revolution!"

"This," Operator 5 echoed grimly, "is revolution—not against our Government, but against your tyranny—not to destroy the United States, but to preserve it from your despotism. I call upon you to hear, President Young, how completely your power is broken tonight. I call upon the nation to listen to evidence of your unutterable perfidy."

OPERATOR 5'S voice rang over the guarded lines, spreading from hundreds of aerials over all the nation.

"At this moment, Mr. President, each member of your Cabinet—puppets, all of them—is a prisoner of the Secret Sentinels. The Vice-President is likewise our captive. They must obey our commands. In a few moments you will learn that they *have* acceded to our demands. And while the nation listens, Mr. President—"

Operator 5 turned; his black-sleeved arm rose to indicate the men and women who had followed him to the platform.

"Look upon the victims of your terrorism! Look upon a few who represent thousands!

"This girl is Diane Elliot, who has served her country, as an unofficial Intelligence operator, more devotedly than any other young woman in the nation. She has continued to work for the preservation of the United States since the beginning of your dictatorship. You chose to construe her opposition to your despotism as treason to her country. For that you sentenced her to death. Tonight you ordered her guillotined! She would not have been the first girl to perish under the blade of your instrument of terror!

"This woman is Mrs. Roger Wentling Marlin, whose son Grant was executed by a firing squad at your order and buried in an unmarked grave outside Hartland—an execution which I witnessed. Scores of other mothers have lost their sons by the guns of your merciless firing squads. Look upon her, President Young—a woman whose son you murdered!"

Young stared malevolently into the calm, grief-stricken eyes of the woman.

"This remnant of a man is William Stockard, once a great newspaper publisher. He is one of the victims of your so-called plague. He was being slowly murdered under your orders— was able only by a desperate effort to escape with his life. He knows, as thousands of your victims now know, President Young, that your plague is one of your weapons of terror, caused by the poisonous medicines fed to your victims by fake doctors under your command. Here, in this bottle, is some of the poison, presented as a cure, which *caused* the deadly epidemic!"

The golden glitter of the liquid in the bottle struck terror into Young's eyes.

"You see standing before you J. Hudson Willing, one of the best beloved men in the United States—and your enemy. This man you ordered stripped of his citizenship and property, and exiled! Beside him stand two women—the wife of a great religious leader, and the wife of a great lawyer—the husbands of these women are being transported at this moment—and by your orders—to a barren island in the center of the Pacific. Look upon the victims of your devilish work, President Young!"

Young stood silent, crushed—knowing that every word uttered was spreading over the entire United States.

"Shall I continue, President Young? Shall I tell the people of the United States how you've confiscated wealth, how you've executed scores of helpless victims without trial, how you've already erected a guillotine for the slaughtering of your enemies, how you've placed the command of the nation's defenses in the hands of corrupt underlings—how you've raided the National Treasury and robbed the poor to whom you promised relief?"

"It's a lie—all of it's a lie!"

At that snarled answer of Young, Operator 5 promptly brought a sheaf of stiff papers from his robe.

"Posing as Lieutenant Doman, an agent of your secret police—" Young's face actually went pasty at the significant words—"I searched your private safe in the White House. I have here photostatic copies of the records I found. These documents show that you have huge accounts in a hundred banks scattered over the Nation. They show that you have huge amounts of cash hidden in a hundred safe-deposit drawers. They prove that year after year you have falsified your income-tax reports and failed to declare the vast sums you acquired by seizure and confiscation. These records show, President Young, how you've tricked the Comptroller of the United States and drawn out of the Federal Treasury huge amounts, to add to your personal loot—a loot which already amounts to millions!"

YOUNG STARED in a paralysis of terror at the damning documents in the hands of Operator 5.

"This is proof, Mr. President, that you are not the noble states-man you have attempted to declare yourself. This is proof that you have, like the scoundrel you are, thieved the people's money!"

Operator 5's eyes flashed through the holes of his cowl as a black-robed figure hurried down the aisle of the hall, past the Senators and Representatives who were listening in cold horror. The messenger ran to Jimmy Christopher's side, passed over a sheaf of documents, and his voice rang.

"The resignations, sir!"

Operator 5 took them into firm hands. "Mr. President, your Cabinet has deserted you. Here are their resignations. Every one of your dummy Cabinet members has resigned, effective at once. The Vice-President has tendered his resignation—it is here. The great departments of this Government are no longer under your control. As for you, sir—"

Jimmy Christopher extended a paper to the President. Young snatched it, stared at it. Operator 5 declared quietly:

"This, sir, is a new appointment you are about to make. It names, as your new Secretary of State, the man you see standing beside me—the man you succeeded as President. It needs only your signature."

Young began, "I refuse—!" and choked off.

"Here," Operator 5 continued quietly, extending another document, "is your own resignation from office. It, too, is ready for your signature. When you affix your name to it, at that moment you will cease to be the Chief Executive—the dictator of the Nation. Automatically your Secretary of State will become President—the man who is now the ex-President will again assume the office which he discharged so nobly."

Young continued to stare at the papers. They seemed to fascinate him.

"We are waiting upon you, sir, to sign that appointment and that resignation!"

Young straightened, his eyes gleaming with fury. But he did not move.

Others did, however. From their chairs about the great hall, Senators and Representatives sprang furiously. Their eyes blazed at the huge figure of the President. Their fists were raised in denunciation.

"Sign them! Sign the papers!"

The voices rose in such a wild and roaring chorus as to stagger Young, cowing him.

"Sign them!"

Ursus Young stood paralyzed.

His first move was to turn to Operator 5. He saw, beneath the gleaming death's-head and the red 5, the darkened eyes of Jimmy Christopher, leveled at him coldly. The power of Operator 5's gaze brought terror to his heart. Suddenly he snatched the pen.

On the paper appointing the ex-President as Secretary of State, he scrawled his signature.

To the document which was his own resignation, he affixed his name as rapidly.

The swift strokes of the pen, in a few seconds, placed the ex-President again at the helm of his great nation.

A CHOKING cry broke from Young's thick lips as he hurled the pen away. He leaped down from the platform, sped along the aisle. A signal from Operator 5 kept the black sentries in their positions. No man moved to stop Young as he rushed toward the doors. His bodyguards trailed after him, cowed by the glittering eyes which watched them. Out of the Hall of Representatives Young raced. He hurried to the entrance of the Capitol; sped out upon the broad portico—and stopped. At the base of the steps, thousands of black-robed men were massed.

A cry of wrath broke from their lips as they glimpsed the hulking figure of the tyrant. They mobbed the steps—an advancing storm of black. Howls of vengeance rose from their throats as Young retreated in terror. He whirled, only to see Sentinels closing in on him from all sides. He found himself in the center of a tightening circle of doom.

Terror seized him. He flew toward the nearest of his bodyguards, snatched the man's weapon. As though bent on a mad attempt to fight everyone at once, he turned, his finger gripping the trigger. And then, again, he retreated when they crowded closer. The gun in his hand was giving them no pause. They came....

Suddenly a blasting shot rang out. Its echoes rattled away beyond the crowd. The closing circle of Sentinels paused. They remained so, their cowled heads bowed, until movement came from the entrance of the Capitol. The black-robed figure marked with the red 5 strode to the center of the cleared space. Operator 5 gazed down.

Ursus Young, resigned President of the United States, lay on the white stone with red blood trickling from a hole in his temple—dead by his own hand.

HISTORY WAS swiftly remade! From the roaring newspaper presses of the nation, from a million radios, the news of the country's rebuilding flashed to the people.

PRESIDENT REAPPOINTS HIS CABINET!

"The General Staffs of the Army and Navy, destroyed by drastic orders of Young while in office, have been restored!"

CORRUPTION OF SUPREME COURT ENDED!

"The Presidential decrees of Young, ladies and gentlemen of the radio audience, are being swiftly wiped out of existence by the new President."

CONSTITUTIONAL RIGHTS RESTORED!

"The secret police of Young are completely disbanded, and all members are imprisoned in Federal Penitentiaries."

BLACK TROOPS DEMOBILIZED! TERROR ENDS!

"All persons victimized by Young's manufactured plague are being treated and it is hoped that they will recover."

CENSORSHIP ENDED! FREE SPEECH RETURNS! NEWSPAPERS AND BROADCASTING STATIONS UNFETTERED! PROPAGANDA ENDS!

"Ladies and gentlemen of the radio audience, the President is working day and night to repair the damages wrought by Young. He is laboring to the limit of his power to re-create the nation. Slowly, stone by stone, the edifice of the United States is being rebuilt. The hindrances to recovery, engineered by Young, are being removed, and prosperity promises an early return. Again the United States is becoming a Government of the people, by the people, and for the people!"

THE DOOR of the secret inner room of the suite of hidden offices, not far from the Capitol, opened slowly. Z-7 stepped into the room which had been his Headquarters. Operator 5 followed; Tim Donovan, John Christopher and Diane Elliot came with him.

They paused, looking around the rooms of WDC-13, which now were empty and still. Young's secret police had been driven from them; but the Intelligence Service had still to be reorganized.

"Your desk, Chief," Jimmy Christopher said quietly. "Yours again!"

Z-7 stepped behind it, and his black eyes lighted with grim joy.

"We have a mighty job ahead of us, my boy—the rebuilding of the entire Intelligence Service. Our agents are scattered; we must call them back. We have to restore our files, our lines of communication. That we have the opportunity to do so—is due to you!"

Operator 5 smiled slowly. "You do me too much honor, Chief. I could never have come back if it hadn't been for Tim. Diane wielded a powerful force with her secret newspaper. Dad's speeches over the hidden radio station prepared the way for our march. Marlin helped—scores of men helped. Thank them, Chief—not me. And most of all—"

The ring of a telephone interrupted. Z-7 took up the instrument. As a voice sounded over the line, he stiffened.

"Yes, Mr. President! He's here!"

He passed the telephone to Operator 5. The voice of the man who had been returned to the White House came over the line ringingly.

"My boy, the work of rebuilding the Nation is a great task—but I must put it aside for the moment to speak to you. I wish you to come to the White House so that I may shake your hand and—"

The voice of the President had grown husky with emotion; now it broke off.

Operator 5 answered quietly: "I will come, Mr. President."

He replaced the phone. His eyes darkened, and a sigh came from his lips.

"Gee, Jimmy!" Tim Donovan exclaimed. "It's true—what

Z-7 said! You did it—you led us all! Gee, Jimmy—I think you're the swellest guy in the world!"

Diane was smiling. "I don't care what anyone else says, Jimmy Christopher—even you. No one will ever find your name recorded in history, and yet you remade the destiny of a nation. Jimmy—I'm so very, very proud of you!"

Operator 5 smiled slowly; and then his smile faded. Z-7 watched him intently. For a moment he seemed lost to his surroundings. His eyes became sad, his mouth pinched. Self-absorbed he stood, until Z-7's quiet question aroused him.

"What are you thinking of, my boy?"

"Of a man who gave his life that our plan might succeed, Chief," Jimmy Christopher answered. "Of a man to whom we owe reverent homage. T-3."

THE BUZZER in the sumptuous penthouse apartment of Carleton Victor sounded, and the redoubtable Crowe, leaving the radio he had just turned on, opened the door. He bowed as Victor entered, brisk in manner and immaculately garbed. Without speaking, Victor gave over his hat, coat and stick.

"If I may say so, sir," Crowe ventured, "you seem tired. The task of making photographs must be a very trying one, sir."

Victor smiled. "Very, Crowe."

Moving toward his desk, he paused. The soft music of the radio had suddenly become blurred. A powerful carrier-wave effaced it—and abruptly a loud voice boomed into the room. Victor stood motionless, listening, eyeing the frowning Crowe.

"Comrades of the Secret Sentinels!" the commanding voice began. "For the last time Headquarters speaks! To all of you, the heartfelt gratitude and esteem of our Chief. Someday we may again be called upon to rise and defend our nation, but now we are safe. Our purpose is accomplished! Our work is done! To all of our loyal soldiers of secrecy—farewell and Godspeed! Farewell!"

The voice vanished. The music returned. Carleton Victor settled into his chair with a sigh. He looked up, curiously, when he heard a disdainful sniff from Crowe.

"Most annoying!" Crowe said.

"I think, Crowe," Victor told him with a chuckle in his words, "that the cause of your annoyance is at an end."

THE SPIDER
- ❏ #1: The Spider Strikes — $13.95
- ❏ #2: The Wheel of Death — $13.95
- ❏ #3: Wings of the Black Death — $13.95
- ❏ #4: City of Flaming Shadows — $13.95
- ❏ #5: Empire of Doom! — $13.95
- ❏ #6: Citadel of Hell — $13.95
- ❏ #7: The Serpent of Destruction — $13.95
- ❏ #8: The Mad Horde — $13.95
- ❏ #9: Satan's Death Blast — $13.95
- ❏ #10: The Corpse Cargo — $13.95
- ❏ #11: Prince of the Red Looters — $13.95
- ❏ #12: Reign of the Silver Terror — $13.95
- ❏ #13: Builders of the Dark Empire — $13.95
- ❏ #14: Death's Crimson Juggernaut — $13.95
- ❏ #15: The Red Death Rain — $13.95
- ❏ #16: The City Destroyer — $13.95
- ❏ #17: The Pain Emperor — $13.95
- ❏ #18: The Flame Master — $13.95
- ❏ #19: Slaves of the Crime Master — $13.95
- ❏ #20: Reign of the Death Fiddler — $13.95
- ❏ #21: Hordes of the Red Butcher — $13.95
- ❏ #22: Dragon Lord of the Underworld — $13.95
- ❏ #23: Master of the Death-Madness — $13.95
- ❏ #24: King of the Red Killers — $13.95
- ❏ #25: Overlord of the Damned — $13.95
- ❏ #26: Death Reign of the Vampire King — $13.95

THE MYSTERIOUS WU FANG
- ❏ #1: The Case of the Six Coffins — $12.95
- ❏ #2: The Case of the Scarlet Feather — $12.95
- ❏ #3: The Case of the Yellow Mask — $12.95
- ❏ #4: The Case of the Suicide Tomb — $12.95
- ❏ #5: The Case of the Green Death — $12.95
- ❏ #6: The Case of the Black Lotus — $12.95
- ❏ #7: The Case of the Hidden Scourge — $12.95

G-8 AND HIS BATTLE ACES
- ❏ #1: The Bat Staffel — $13.95

CAPTAIN SATAN
- ❏ #1: The Mask of the Damned — $13.95
- ❏ #2: Parole for the Dead — $13.95
- ❏ #3: The Dead Man Express — $13.95
- ❏ #4: A Ghost Rides the Dawn — $13.95
- ❏ #5: The Ambassador From Hell — $13.95

CAPTAIN ZERO
- ❏ #1: City of Deadly Sleep — $13.95
- ❏ #2: The Mark of Zero! — $13.95
- ❏ #3: The Golden Murder Syndicate — $13.95

OPERATOR 5
- ❏ #1: The Masked Invasion — $13.95
- ❏ #2: The Invisible Empire — $13.95
- ❏ #3: The Yellow Scourge — $13.95
- ❏ #4: The Melting Death — $13.95
- ❏ #5: Cavern of the Damned — $13.95
- ❏ #6: Master of Broken Men — $13.95
- ❏ #7: Invasion of the Dark Legions — $13.95
- ❏ #8: The Green Death Mists — $13.95
- ❏ #9: Legions of Starvation — $13.95
- ❏ #10: The Red Invader — $13.95
- ❏ #11: The League of War-Monsters — $13.95
- ❏ #12: The Army of the Dead — $13.95
- ❏ #13: March of the Flame Marauders — $13.95
- ❏ *NEW:* #14: Blood Reign of the Dictator — $13.95

DUSTY AYRES AND HIS BATTLE BIRDS
- ❏ #1: Black Lightning! — $13.95
- ❏ #2: Crimson Doom — $13.95
- ❏ #3: The Purple Tornado — $13.95
- ❏ #4: The Screaming Eye — $13.95
- ❏ #5: The Green Thunderbolt — $13.95
- ❏ #6: The Red Destroyer — $13.95
- ❏ #7: The White Death — $13.95
- ❏ #8: The Black Avenger — $13.95
- ❏ #9: The Silver Typhoon — $13.95
- ❏ #10: The Troposphere F-S — $13.95
- ❏ #11: The Blue Cyclone — $13.95
- ❏ #12: The Tesla Raiders — $13.95

DR. YEN SIN
- ❏ #1: Mystery of the Dragon's Shadow — $12.95
- ❏ #2: Mystery of the Golden Skull — $12.95
- ❏ #3: Mystery of the Singing Mummies — $12.95

MAVERICKS
- ❏ #1: Five Against the Law — $12.95
- ❏ #2: Mesquite Manhunters — $12.95
- ❏ #3: Bait for the Lobo Pack — $12.95
- ❏ #4: Doc Grimson's Outlaw Posse — $12.95
- ❏ #5: Charlie Parr's Gunsmoke Cure — $12.95